"An erotic thriller which sets new moral boundaries."—*Abilene Reporter-News*

"A story of urban and moral decay as accurate and disturbing as *Bonfire of the Vanities*."—Nelson DeMille

"An engaging story . . . Segal knows the Big Apple milieu well . . . she has written an involving tale."—*New Bedford Standard Times*

"Segal can write!"—*South Bend Tribune*

With this poignant and powerful novel, Kathrin King Segal gives vivid focus to the inscene dynamic of the 1990's. The world of Art and Margo—at once glittering and crumbling, meaningful and hedonistic, and inescapably dangerous—emerges as a microcosm of contemporary urban life. *Wild Again* marks a debut of spectacular achievement.

DRAMA & ROMANCE

(0451)

☐ **FLOWERS OF BETRAYAL by June Triglia.** Tiziana D'Eboli risked everything to free herself from a ruthless mafia bond. Here is a novel of passion, shame, deceit, and murder—and the stunning woman who took destiny into her own hands. (402472—$5.99)

☐ **BOUND BY BLOOD by June Triglia.** Two beautiful sisters overcome brutal pasts to become successful and prominent women. From Pittsburgh to Paris, from Manhattan to Milan, Angie and Nickie learn just how far they can go. "Masterful storytelling that will keep you turning pages!"—Fred Mustard Stewart (401832—$4.95)

☐ **ENTICEMENTS by Una-Mary Parker.** "Glitz and murder . . . on the cutting edge between Ruth Rendell and Judith Krantz."—*Chicago Tribune* (170997—$5.50)

☐ **VEIL OF SECRETS by Una-Mary Parker.** In this sizzling novel of mystery and seduction, Una-Mary Parker vividly interweaves the *haut monde* with affairs of art and finance, giving full reign to three beautiful women who become tangled in a triangle of love, passion and greed. "A glitzy romp with the rich and famous."—*Booklist* (169328—$4.99)

☐ **DOCTORS AND DOCTORS' WIVES by Francis Roe.** Greg Hopkins and Willie Stringer, two powerful and dedicated doctors, find their friendship shattered by personal and professional rivalries. A masterful medical drama, this novel vividly portrays the lives and loves of doctors and their fascinating, high-pressure world. (169107—$5.50)

WILD AGAIN

Kathrin King Segal

AN ONYX BOOK

ONYX
Published by the Penguin Group
Penguin Books USA Inc., 375 Hudson Street,
New York, New York 10014, U.S.A.
Penguin Books Ltd, 27 Wrights Lane,
London W8 5TZ, England
Penguin Books Australia Ltd, Ringwood,
Victoria, Australia
Penguin Books Canada Ltd, 10 Alcorn Avenue
Toronto, Ontario, Canada M4V 3B2
Penguin Books (N.Z.) Ltd, 182-190 Wairau Road,
Auckland 10, New Zealand

Penguin Books Ltd, Registered Offices:
Harmondsworth, Middlesex, England

Published by Onyx, an imprint of New American Library, a division of Penguin
Books USA Inc. Previously published in a Dutton edition.

First Onyx Printing, April, 1992
10 9 8 7 6 5 4 3 2 1

Grateful acknowledgment is made for permission to reprint the following:

Excerpt from "Song for the Last Act" from *The Blue Estuaries* by Louise Bogan.
Copyright © 1949 by Louise Bogan. Renewal copyright © 1976 by Maidie Alexander
Scannell. Reprinted by permission of Farrar, Straus & Giroux, Inc.

Excerpt from "Pictures of a Gone World" from Lawrence Ferlinghetti: *A Coney
Island of the Mind*, Copyright © 1958 by Lawrence Ferlinghetti. Reprinted by
permission of New Directions Publishing Corporation. World rights.

Excerpt from "Beyond the Sea" English lyric by Jack Lawrence. Music and French
lyric by Charles Trenet. © 1945 Editions Raoul Breton. © Renewed 1973 Charles
Trenet. © 1947 T.B. Harms. © Renewed 1975 MPL Communications, Inc.
International Copyright Secured. All Rights Reserved.

Excerpt from "One for My Baby (And One More for the Road)" Lyric by Johnny
Mercer. Music by Harold Arlen. © 1943 Harwin Music Co. © Renewed 1971 Harwin
Music Co. International Copyright Secured. All Rights Reserved.

Excerpt from "La Chanson des Vieux Amants" (Jacques Brel, Gerard Jouannest)
© 1969 Pouchenel, Editions. All rights administered by Unichappell Music Inc. All
Rights Reserved. Used By Permission.

Excerpt from "Send In The Clowns" © 1973 Stephen Sondheim. Revelation Music
Publishing Corp/Rilting Music Inc. A Tommy Valando Publication.

Title "Pretty Women" © 1978 Stephen Sondheim. Revelation Music Publishing
Corp/Rilting Music Inc. A Tommy Valando Publication.

PUBLISHER'S NOTE
This is a work of fiction. Names, characters, places, and incidents either are the
product of the author's imagination or are used fictitiously, and any resemblance
to actual persons, living or dead, events, or locales is entirely coincidental.

for Steve

ACKNOWLEDGMENTS

My deepest appreciation to Phyllis Levy for her boundless generosity, love, and support.

Also, and especially: Anne Carey, Charles Brown, and Bill Turner.

To my agent, Malaga Baldi, and editor, Audrey LaFehr.

And special thanks to my Writers Group: Neil Alers, Susan E. Davis, and Robert Fisher.

Now that I have your voice by heart, I read
In the black chords upon a dulling page
Music that is not meant for music's cage,
Whose emblems mix with words that shake
    and bleed.
The staves are shuttled over with a stark
Unprinted silence. In a double dream
I must spell out the storm, the running
    stream.
The beat's too swift. The notes shift in the
    dark.
          —Louise Bogan, "Song for the Last Act"

    The world is a beautiful place
                              to be born into
If you don't mind happiness
                    not always being
                         so very much fun
if you don't mind a touch of hell
                         now and then
        just when everything is fine
                         because even in heaven
              they don't sing
                         all the time
                    —Lawrence Ferlinghetti,
                    "Pictures of a Gone World"

PROLOGUE

He had done some terrible thing and now he was lost.

Pivoting to the right, he pushed his hand out into black space to regain his balance and grasped leaves, palm fronds. The moon slid out from behind a cloud and he began to see where he was, high atop a hill overlooking the island. He heard the dull throbbing of his heart and knew, just then, that a heart did not so much break as shatter, like a car window crystallized on impact.

It felt as if the nightmare had been going on forever, but it was only a matter of days since he had stood over her lifeless body and felt his world tilt. Yet his flight from that world had not brought him peace or safety and had only driven him to run again.

He stood still in the dark tropical night, willing his heart to slow its painful beating, and tried to focus his mind. He was just beginning to feel calmer when he heard the distant cold howling, a long drawn-out cry that was both animal and human, as if all the loss and loveless pain of the world had been given a pure, aching voice.

1

Art placed the brandy glass on top of the piano and thrust a five-dollar bill into it, to give customers the right idea. Balancing a lit cigarette on the ashtray, he flexed his fingers, hands poised over the gleaming keys. He took a deep breath of boozy, smoky air and played the first chords to his jazzy arrangement of "Always," then segued into "Always on My Mind" and "All Alone." After almost two years of playing four hours a night—when he showed up—he used tricks to keep himself interested, like selecting his songs alphabetically. At least that way if he lost track of the time and he was playing "Younger Than Springtime," he'd know the night was nearly over.

It was a little after ten and the crowd at Jack's Café-Bar was crossing over: the after-work suits clearing out, staggering home to their tiny, overpriced co-ops, and the hipper late-night set arriving, casing the joint with cooler-than-thou deadpan faces.

Owner Jack Brady strode in, half a head taller than anyone else, an Irishman from Brooklyn who still spoke with the streety old neighborhood accent, his nose permanently tilted from ancient brawls. He'd started in the saloon business thirty years before, a bar with a shamrock on a green neon sign, then caught the wave of singles in the late sixties with a hangout on upper First Avenue. When the West Side turned trendy, he opened a second place, added a cocktail pianist, and had it done in peach and chrome and glass, huge carnivorous-looking plants hanging overhead. The menu, once hearty stews and burger fare from sweaty steam tables and greasy grills, was now a light and expensive mélange of chèvre and endive salads, catch of the day, and baked potato skins.

Art could scarcely hear himself as he turned into the microphone to sing the words to "Bewitched, Bothered and Bewildered." Jack was roaring behind the bar, mixing drinks because he did it faster than the harried bartender, keeping an eye on the front door for unsavories and Bridge and Tunnels.

Art liked to throw in a "Danny Boy" every so often for Jack, and he made a mental note to sing it tonight, when he got to the D's. Jack loved whatever Art sang, which was no compliment really, since Jack admittedly had a tin ear. He just liked listening to the guy play the piano, and the customers kept coming back, so Art Glenn must be doing something right.

Art looked up from the piano and caught Jack's salute, a mock salaam of gratitude for the bar's swarming crowds. Art thought Jack gave him too much credit, that the place would pack 'em in even if there was a performing monkey at a toy piano, because for now Jack's was the hot spot, and next year it would be someplace else. Art used to like it when Jack's was a little less successful and the customers could hear the songs, but he'd quickly gotten over that kind of nostalgia as the tips filled the glass night after night, all that nice, crisp, off-the-books cash.

The extra weekend waiter, Desmond, was on tonight, an aspiring singer-dancer who scurried around announcing the specials at his tables as if he were auditioning for an entire Broadway season. Every so often, just before closing, when the only customers left were too strung out to care, Jack persuaded Art to let Desmond sing a few tunes. The kid would excitedly press some tattered sheet music in front of Art and grab the extra microphone.

"Good evening and welcome to Jack's, the crème de la crème on the Upper West Side! Is everybody happy!"

Yeah, sure. Right. Could you bring my order?

"I'm your singing waiter! I sing, you wait!" He'd burst into song, with Art dutifully accompanying, wondering how he'd gotten to this particular place in his life.

Playing the piano was something he had picked up by ear as a kid, at first as a game to impress his mother with imitations of the songs she sang.

She was a singer with a perky Teresa Brewer sound who played small hotel lounges and clubs throughout the country. The Big Break was a perpetual carrot luring her ever onward. Lila Noone had been born Lottie Lefkowitz in Brooklyn, New York, and left her family's small, neat apartment in Flatbush for the wilds of Manhattan when she was sixteen. She planned to become a star right away and changed her name to Lila Lord, which her family thought was insultingly goyish. She kept auditioning for chorus jobs but didn't have a big enough voice or sufficient skill as a dancer. Instead, she worked as a waitress until she was fired for offending a customer to whom she'd brought the wrong order—Lila had trouble with things like apologies—and took a job posing in negligees for amateur photographers in a run-down Times Square loft. Eventually she hooked up with a lounge band called the Star Five and joined them on the road as their sequin-clad chick singer. By this time she'd been briefly married to Frank E. Noone, an earnest Bronx plumber, and taken both his name and his baby son with her when she left him.

Art couldn't recall his father in any real sense, and as far as he knew, Frank Noone had never sought him out either. Art's most vivid memory of those early years was of lying on a bed staring at a painting on what must have been some motel-room wall. The picture was just a watercolor of a city skyline, but to him it represented that one place where they might finally come to rest in their perpetual journey.

He was a quirky, good-looking boy, with slightly crooked front teeth and dark-lashed golden-hazel eyes that girls began to call "bedroom" before he knew what they meant. He was awkwardly shy, except when he sat down at the piano. Then he was transformed. He got better and better, finding lots of time to practice while waiting for his mother in countless Starlight Rooms and Peacock Lounges and Eddie's Niteries. The music came pouring out through his fingertips, into poignant renditions of the purest love songs or nervously intense jazz improvisations. He developed a clean singing style, a little Mose Allison warmed by Sinatra.

Art scanned the room as he played, surveying the women. He took a deep drag of his cigarette, a sip of Jack Daniel's, and selected a self-assured streaked blonde who was talking to another woman, less attractive. They were both young, looked like ad-agency slaves who spent the day thinking up annoying commercials people zapped with their remotes. He turned back to the keys. "Blue Skies." "Come Rain or Come Shine." She was looking at him now, as if she'd just discovered he was alive and not an audioanimatronic from Disney World, and he knew how easy it would be. Piano players were so romantic, they all told him.

At "Every Breath You Take" she excused herself to her friend and approached. In a fast-forward mental videotape he lived the night in the time it took her to cross the room: a quick medley of bare skin, the exchange of verbal résumés, textures and scents, and the letdown when he discovered she was not going to resolve his life and that he'd actually have to deal with her. ("Yes, honey, I'll give you a call," keeping the number on a scrap of paper in his pocket until it faded or he couldn't remember whose number it was.) She leaned close, draping herself over the piano to show her cleavage, and promised to wait till the last set was done at two. She was cute enough, her bare shoulder as lickable as a scoop of vanilla Sedutto.

When Art was twelve, his mother had an extended engagement in Cleveland, playing at Forrester's Inn out on the highway that passed by vast Lake Erie. Lila called the town "the mistake on the lake." Cold November winds swept across the parking lot late at night when they climbed into their old white Chrysler for the short drive from the motel to the club, Lila shivering in her glamorous gown beneath a shedding rabbit-fur coat. It took a while for Art to realize that the main reason they were sticking around Cleveland was Charley Forrester, the club's owner. He was a small, thin man who wore plaid sports jackets and was always accompanied by a pair of sleek black Doberman pinschers named Diablo and Diego.

When Art was younger, Lila would put him to bed before she went off to work so that they could do his bedtime routine. Lila would pretend he was still very, very small, hold him in her arms, and recite: "I love you in all the warm and sunny places in the universe. I love you in all the planets and the stars." Art would repeat this back to her until they both dissolved into giggles, Lila would kiss him, turn out the light, and leave.

Somewhere along the way, Art had outgrown the bedtime ritual and he stayed back at the motel trying to keep up with schoolwork from the latest new school. With the TV blaring in the background, he tried to muster up some interest in history and math but found himself more often tapping out tunes with his fingers, wishing there was a piano under them. He liked to go to the club in the late afternoon and play before the place got busy, ignored by the couple of drunk salesmen getting a head start on the night, hookers in pastel miniskirts and hair that ballooned up like cotton-candy poofs before cascading down in ironed sheets. He'd hang out unobtrusively until it was time for his mother's first set because it was better than staying alone, even though lately she paid more attention to Charley Forrester. He got the feeling that Charley liked to pretend that Lila didn't have a son at all, that maybe she was really only twenty-five and had never been married. She went along with the game, giggling and calling Art her "little brother," one time saying that he was "the drummer's kid" as a joke.

Charley's dogs, Diablo and Diego, frightened Art, growling low whenever he came near. Being on the road so much, Art was unused to dogs or pets of any kind. Once, he'd found a kitten near the Holiday Inn somewhere in Indiana, and he'd snuck it into their room until Lila found out and put it outside again. She didn't like animals in the house, she yelled, especially cats. They were sneaky and you never knew what they were thinking. And also, she added, to mollify him, it wasn't fair to the animal to get it attached to them when they'd only have to leave it behind.

One day, she promised, they'd settle down and have all the animals he could ever want.

It was in Cleveland that Lila started favoring rock songs because she said that was the only way she was going to get a recording contract. And a hit record was the only way she could get off the lounge circuit. Charley, she said, had connections in the music business and was going to help her. So she was doing Beatles medleys and Rolling Stones and Creedence

Clearwater Revival, but all that top-forty stuff sounded thin and ineffectual when played by the Star Five and sung by "songstress" Lila Noone, who'd been raised on the lush pop songs of the forties and fifties. She no longer sang Art's favorites, not even the song that had been her standby for years, "Bewitched, Bothered and Bewildered."

Now, when the occasional young party came to Forrester's, Art saw them smirking behind their drinks. It made him sad, then angry, that his mother didn't even know what she should be singing, after all these years. And there she was, no longer a kid but a slightly overweight woman in her midthirties, spilling out of her dress and gushing "Proud Mary" into the microphone. Suddenly he hated her with a rage that took him by surprise.

He got up abruptly and went outside, a cruel blast of icy snow stinging his face. He stayed there for a long time, hearing the set-ending music from the bandstand, and Lila's cheery "We'll be taking a break right now but we'll be right back, so keep on having a happy time!" to the dozen or so straggly customers.

He waited for her to notice he was missing, to come outside looking for him, but he only got colder and colder. Hurting from it, he went back inside to tell her he was going to call a taxi and go back to the motel. She wasn't at the bar or in the lobby, or at any of the tables where customers often bought her a drink between sets. He slumped down on the hideous floraled sofa in the area where people waited to be seated and picked up a drink someone had left there. He sucked on a piece of Scotch-tinged ice and waited.

Restless, he got up again and walked into the lobby. As he passed by the door marked "Manager's Office," he stopped. Maybe his mother was in there talking to Charley Forrester. He knocked and walked in.

For a moment he was confused. His mother was kneeling down as if she'd dropped an earring, but Charley wasn't helping her look for it. He was sitting on a chair with his pants undone. They both looked up, faces pink and surprised.

"What the fuck . . . ?" said Charley.

The two dogs flanked both sides of the desk, like gargoyles. They stood as one, growling so deep in their throats Art felt more than heard the vibration.

He did not know exactly what had happened except that it was bad and he could see only the glittering black eyes of the dogs. He ran out, his hand over his mouth, and made it to the parking lot, where he threw up everything he'd eaten and drunk that whole day and night.

In a few minutes he felt her hand on his back. He shrugged her off, curling himself into a ball until he could feel the gravel of the parking lot scraping his arms. She leaned closer, crouching down, her long dress in folds around her legs.

"Artie, I know you don't understand, but you will when you're older. Sometimes your mama just gets lonely. You know what I mean, honey? And she needs a friend, a man to help her feel better. And when you're grown up, that means a . . . uh . . . different kind of thing than when you're a child. And maybe I used bad judgment but it's this crazy life and I know it's my fault but one of these days, when I've got a hit song and we've got our place, you'll forget all about this. And that day, honey, is sooner than you think—"

"No, it isn't." He sat up, the gravel still sticking to his face and hands. He picked it off, one pebble at a time. "No, it is never going to happen the way you say because you're not good enough."

"What?" She sat back, as if struck.

He didn't know where the coldness came from but he heard himself saying the words, like icy stones dropped into a deep pool. "You're never going to have a hit record. You stink! And I hate you and hate you in all the cold icy places in the universe. I'll hate you forever."

He got up and went inside, leaving her sitting on the ground.

He started walking down the driveway to the main road. The world would come to an end soon, he thought.

A car pulled up beside him and a stringy young guy rolled down the window and asked if he was Arthur Noone. He nodded.

"Well, Forrester sent me to find you and get you back to your motel."

Without a word Art got in the dented Valiant. They drove in silence until they reached the motel, only a few miles down the highway. Art didn't make a move to get out.

"So, this is it, right?" asked the driver.

Art didn't reply.

"I'm Vinnie. I work for Charley Forrester, odd jobs, you know? So listen, you smoke?"

Art shrugged.

Vinnie pulled out a joint and lit up, passed it over to Art. He'd never smoked pot before but he knew what it was, from the guys in the band. He and Vinnie sat in the parking lot, passing it back and forth. The car windows fogged up from their breath and the smoke, until Art couldn't see anything outside except for the blurred light from the motel sign, blinking on and off. The pot didn't do much for him, except make him feel headachy and tired.

After a while, he said good night to Vinnie, got out of the car, and went inside the room. Clothes and makeup, books and magazines, his and Lila's, littered the room but he didn't pick anything up. He cleared his bed by sliding everything into a pile on the floor. The only thing on TV after midnight was a preacher signing off with warnings about eternal damnation. Art searched the room's midget refrigerator, finding instant coffee, soured milk, and an opened bottle of flat champagne. He drank it, mixed with ice from the ice machine across the hall, and fell asleep in the room's one chair.

He awoke with a start at dawn, alone. His mother had not come back all night. A headache throbbed behind his eyes. The TV murmured "Sunrise Semester." The words to a song floated through his mind, something about a lavender morning but he couldn't recall if he'd heard it or made it up in his dreams. He drifted off again, until a sharp knock on the door startled him out of sleep, his heart pounding.

Years later, when he thought about that night and the hard dawn that followed, changing his life forever, it seemed as if all the events had been something he'd seen in a movie or a television show, a film that had gone blank in the middle, and when he awoke it was sometime later and he was on a bus alone heading to New York City. He was nearly thirteen years old and he was going to live with people he'd never even met, and all he could think about was how long it would be until he was old enough to get away from all of them.

He stayed awake through the long night bus ride, leafing through a Pittsburgh newspaper some passenger had left behind and read about John Glenn, who had just resigned from the astronaut team. Art had only been four when Glenn orbited the earth, but he saw the pictures on television and his mother explained to him that a man was flying around out there in space. Art felt a leap in his body, as in the dreams he often had, where he stepped off a curb and began to soar, higher and higher until he was far above the highways and motels and could see his mother's tired white Chrysler gliding along the road below like a marble.

Art went to live with his mother's elderly parents in their Flatbush apartment. Once he got to New York, thin and exhausted from the long bus ride and all that had happened, he thought he recalled being there before, even though he knew he had been an infant at the time and couldn't possibly remember.

His father, Frank Noone, was remarried and had a large family of his own and no interest in the son he'd never seen, by the woman who'd dumped him so long ago.

Gramma Rose and Grampa Morty were perfectly nice people who had little energy left for an adolescent boy. They tried to get him to attend school regularly, something he'd never before experienced and didn't particularly enjoy. He had trouble being in the same place day after day, sitting still and having to pay attention. Every once in a while, when he'd disappointed them again, one would turn to the other and say in a hushed voice, "The apple doesn't fall far from the tree." For a long time he got this mixed up with the story of Adam and Eve.

The grandparents wanted him to go to college, to find a real profession, but he couldn't sit at a desk or in an office. It was only when he played the piano that he really came to life.

* * *

He took a sip of Jack Daniel's, a little too diluted from melting ice, but the sharp sweet sting was good, focusing his senses. The faces, noise, smoke swirled around him and he felt a surge of elation, for being alive and pulsing with sexual energy and because he was thirty-two and his hairline showed not the slightest sign of thinning. Okay, so maybe he should be farther along, especially when he thought about Mozart dying at thirty-five, Gershwin at thirty-eight. Of course, lately *everyone* was dying young, so some of the cachet had worn off. But he was taut and feral and could be anyone he wanted to be. That was why he was Art Glenn and not pathetic little Arthur Noone.

"How's it going, Art?" asked Desmond, brushing by, a tray held aloft.

"Great, kiddo. Could use another of these." He tapped his drink glass.

"Coming right up," Desmond promised. "Listen, I have some friends coming later. Do you think maybe I could do a couple of songs? Please?"

"Sure, guy," he answered, feeling magnanimous. "Some Wagner, a little Verdi? Manilow?"

"*Right.*" Desmond grinned happily and hurried to the bar to get Art's refill. Art closed out his set and took a break, heading first to the cigarette machine and then to the men's room.

"Arthur, long time, no call." She stopped him just outside the door, a petite young woman with short brown hair and wide dark eyes, and he remembered that she had small firm breasts with nipples like little copper pennies. He recalled them but not her name.

"Honey, my schedule's been crazy. Working here. Playing parties. Writing songs. No time for social life. I didn't forget."

"Well, maybe I'll forgive you this time." Her eyes were too bright from doing lines in the bathroom, which reminded him of the lost night and day he'd spent with her.

"I'll call ya," he said, pushing open the door to the sanctuary of the toilet. He took a leak, splashed a little water on his face, and lit a cigarette. What the hell was her name anyway?

Back at the piano, the time passed tolerably. Ones and fives and the occasional ten filled his tip glass. Some joker put in a Canadian dime.

"Those Were the Days, My Friend," he sang, segued into an instrumental "While We're Young" and presently "At the Zoo," which wasn't really a Z song but he liked it.

He waved at the blonde who had waited till closing, got his jacket from the storeroom behind the kitchen, where the noise was muffled, the air damp and redolent of old beer. He sat for a moment on an unopened carton of beer nuts, the sudden quiet like a pressure against his ears.

In her apartment, he started to ask for a drink but she shushed him impatiently with a kiss. The convertible sofa in her small studio was open, as if she'd just gotten out of it, sheets and blankets askew. She was busily unbuckling his pants and he was about to reach for the packet of condoms in his wallet when she jumped the gun, so to speak, and produced one from her mouth. When did she slip it in, or did she have it there all along, like chewing gum? She tugged him to the floor, twisting around so that she faced his legs. She'd shed most of her clothes along the way, revealing Calvin Klein women's jocks. These she slid down and off, keeping him in her mouth as she went. He nearly lost his erection in his admiration of her dexterity, rather inclined to give her a round of applause. Just before she guided him into sixty-nine position, she slipped a piece of Saran Wrap over her parts, and thrust up into his face, fully sanitized. He couldn't remember ever going down on plastic before, but there was a first time for everything.

2

Margo Magill stood at the corner of Fifty-seventh Street and Lexington Avenue, unsure what to do with the rest of her evening. A light autumn rain was falling and she didn't have an umbrella. A few feet away, an ebony-skinned man crouched on an upturned carton box and called out " 'brella! 'brella!" over and over, proffering a handful of black collapsibles made in Taiwan. It didn't seem worth it to spend four dollars when she had several perfectly good umbrellas in her apartment closet, but of course they were of no use just then. The thought made her eyes fill with tears, as if the umbrellas were neglected pets she'd forgotten to walk.

She had wanted to go to Bloomingdale's, but when she got there, after staying late at work to tend to an emergency admission, the store was closing. It had been a strange and confusing day, the patients she'd seen were stacked up in her mind, crowding her with their endless needs and problems.

A twenty-three-year-old black woman, abused by her father, then by her boyfriend, with three children in foster homes, burned out of her tenement, living in a shelter and sent to Bellevue Psychiatric when she became disruptive. As a psychiatric social worker, Margo did the evaluations, made recommendations to the doctors, and tried to figure out how to fit these flotsam people into a system that couldn't or wouldn't handle them.

Margo had found the woman surprisingly easy to talk to, her anger understandable: at the red tape she endured each day trying to get food, a place to sleep, clean clothing. Yet the woman was not sick enough for admission nor stable enough to extricate herself from her downward spiral. Margo sent her upstairs to see a psychiatrist, knowing that all they would do was dole out a prescription for tranquilizers or antidepressants and send her back out to the streets.

Another case saddened her more: an alcoholic man in his fifties who once had a flourishing acting career (he pulled out a soiled old clipping to show her). For a moment she thought she might take him home, give him a real meal and a real bed, and save him. But she sent him to detox for a few days, knowing he would be drinking again as soon as he was out.

Now she was restless, awash with nameless

feelings and a vague sexual longing. She rarely dated anymore. It was always such a disappointment, but she had been cajoled into accepting a date the next night with the accountant who came to the hospital every month to do the books. It wasn't that she was particularly attracted to him—that kind of chemical attraction only ended badly anyway, and took too much out of you. Perhaps a nice, boring guy was what she needed. And so she had agreed to go with him on his company's anniversary cruise, a festive evening's sail around Manhattan on a chartered yacht. She'd had the vague idea of finding something new and wonderful to wear, but the rain and her fatigue and the closed Bloomingdale's had put an end to that fantasy.

This was the kind of night when her thoughts turned to Michael. Whenever she began thinking about Michael, she knew depression was not far behind. Even though it had been over for more than a decade, he lingered in a corner of her mind. Sometimes she wanted to be back with him, no matter how terrible the emotional cost, if only to feel that way again, that ecstasy of mind and body without past or future. Perhaps it was merely a time in her life she longed for.

She began walking west, catching glimpses of herself in drizzly store windows, a pretty, slim woman with soft light blond hair darkened by the rain, in a droopy gray raincoat and well-worn running sneakers. She paused at the Chanel window, distracted by an exquisite, beaded black purse. She went in, the thick glass doors barely whispering her entrance. A lithe saleswoman, no more than twenty-five, slithered over, offering assistance in a skeptical voice. Margo, immediately self-conscious, mumbled that she was only browsing. She spotted the purse and surreptitiously turned over its tiny price tag: $850. Swallowing, avoiding the bored stare of the saleswoman, she slipped out silently and continued walking in the rain.

At thirty-seven, Margo was experiencing a profound existential bewilderment. She had drifted through her youthful years, following this dream and that, certain that everything would fall into place eventually. She'd grown up in a blue-collar section of Schenectady, New York, a town close enough to the more glittering capital of Albany and the society hub of Saratoga Springs to feel the contrast. At least Margo grew up feeling it, because her mother had instilled in her at an early age the conviction that they were better than their neighbors. Her mother's family had been wealthy at one time, but lost it all in the Crash, living on memories ever after. When Margo's mother married a construction man, she had seen him as an exotic species, the physical man, the John Wayne of her high school. She believed that he would rise above his origins, take over the construction company for which he worked, and climb the American entrepreneurial ladder. But Margo's father had no such ambitions, nor the imagination to conceive of them.

She'd gotten out of Schenectady on a scholarship to NYU, drifting through the theater department before majoring in English literature. She supported herself as a waitress all through college and long after she graduated, a useless bachelor of liberal arts. She shared an apartment with two other actresses on the pregentrified Upper West Side, worked occasionally, mostly in off-off-Broadway and experimental theater companies where money was scarce. She rolled around on the floor wailing with a Grotowski-inspired company that put on abrasive antiestablishment plays in basements and churches. Margo found it hard to balance this life with the necessary business side of show business. She hated calling agents and casting directors, waiting hours and hours to be seen for maybe thirty seconds. It seemed commercial and crass and demeaning. By 1980, she was not working at all at her craft. She was, as far as the world was concerned, a waitress. She was also divorced.

Michael was the one everybody knew was going to make it. Even in the small ensemble theater company where they met, Michael stood out. He was the one agents called while all the other actors were futilely calling those same agents day after day, just trying to get in for an appointment. Michael swaggered into a room, brimming with confidence, a cigarette in the corner of his mouth like a young Bogart, an endearing wisecrack on his lips. On his first day of rehearsal, cast as the ardent, doomed Roger in the company's production of Genet's *The Balcony* (Margo had the small role of the Penitent), Michael, wearing round dark glasses and strikingly chic, thrift-shop clothes, intrigued the women and irritated the men.

In time, the wiser women slept with him for fun and moved on, or simply steered clear, but Margo had no such wisdom. Although she saw him flash the same smile at the theater interns, the director's wife, the girl at the box office, every once in a while he looked at her with such open sweetness, shrugging as if to say "I know I'm a louse, love me anyway," that in no time at all she did. Rehearsals became the center of her world, and she was acutely aware of Michael, as if she had grown some invisible antenna that tracked him constantly, monitored his presence. If he sat next to another actress, she mourned; if she heard him laughing in conversation with someone else, she could barely concentrate on what she was doing.

Some nights, watching from the back of the house as he rehearsed his erotic scenes with the actress playing Chantal, she had to leave the theater and stand in the winter air, the searing cold a preferable pain to her sick, roiling jealousy. She could not eat or sleep, and by the end of the week she had a raging fever and was out of rehearsal for two days.

Lying in bed in the cluttered, cramped apartment she shared with two equally slovenly roommates, taking a slow-working antibiotic because she was toxically allergic to penicillin, she fantasized-hallucinated about Michael. Her brain seemed to have stuck like a scratched record, replaying him over and over. When she had recovered, pale and thin, her waist-length silver-blond hair nearly blending with her white skin, she returned to the theater, which was a converted carriage house on East Sixth Street. The first person she saw was Michael, studying his lines aloud in the small lobby.

"Hey, it's Camille back on her feet," he said, the ever-present cigarette in the corner of his mouth. "Didn't you ever hear about 'the show must go on'?"

She was shaky from the illness, even more so from seeing him again, and he noticed her hands trembling. He put his arm around her shoulders and led her to a chair. "Take it easy, you Aryan beauty you," he said softly. He went out to the deli and brought her back a pint of orange juice and a hot tea with lemon and wrapped his scarf around her neck.

After rehearsal ended, he took her to his place. She was shocked. Instead of the usual actor's tenement with a passel of roommates, Michael lived in a stately old building overlooking Gramercy Park. He explained that it was a sublet, a friend of a family friend's. The apartment was not huge, having only one bedroom, but it was airy and elegant. There was a working fireplace in the living room. Michael set Margo up in front of it, wrapping a hand-crocheted afghan around her, bringing her more tea, putting on a record of mellow Miles Davis. He asked her about her life, where she was from, what she liked to do.

"Am I boring you?" she asked after a long recital of her family history.

"Sure, kiddo," he joked. "You know how I drift off when I'm not talking about myself."

His hand touched lightly behind her neck, and she was aware of her body leaning into his. She had had enough sexual experiences in college and after, one relationship that had lasted six months, but she had never, she realized at that moment, really been in love, or so sexually aroused.

"I want to tell you how I feel," he said, "but I'm not really good at this. I mean, I can flirt and carry on, but I guess I'm a little emotionally backward." He poured himself another Scotch, sat down again, and stroked her hair. He amused her with a story of his first audition in New York, how he'd had to learn dance steps even though he was no dancer. When he shifted his hips slightly to demonstrate, she felt a ripple of sexual sensation shudder within her. She closed her eyes, waiting for it to pass, like a tiny earthquake that momentarily stops life from moving forward. When she opened her eyes, he had stopped speaking and was looking at her, as if he knew. He leaned over and kissed her, once, twice on the lips, and then they were making love. She was coming even before he entered her, again when he did, and later when he kissed her and tongued her into a near blackout of sparkling lights and stars.

She began staying over at his place more often, moving her things in gradually. Michael agreed that it would make more sense if she just moved in completely, so she gave up her roommate slot in the shabby apartment on West Ninety-seventh, and joined Michael.

He proposed after an opening-night party of the company's well-received neo-performance-art production of Ionesco's *The Bald Soprano*, which had an electronic music score and large puppets representing the alter egos of the characters. They were married a week later at City Hall.

She was so amazed, so flattered that he loved her. She wondered why, and often asked him. He always answered her playfully, "Because you're the perfect blond shiksa. All over." Or, "Because you laugh at my jokes." Once, he said, "Because you love *me* so much."

Michael's career was starting to take off in small, important ways. He landed a tiny role in a film, a week's shoot in New York and a chance to work with top stars and director. That was followed by a guest spot on a "Kojak" episode, and then another movie, a bigger part this time. While Margo toiled away building sets, sewing costumes, and performing small roles in the theater group, Michael came home talking about agents and contracts and how he was "on hold" for a Burger King spot and up for a new play at Manhattan Theatre Club. Yet, as he became more in demand, rather than enjoying his success, he grew tense and angry.

She was patient. She had seen her mother put up with her father's rages for years and knew how to lay low, to try to say the right thing or nothing at all, to stay out of his way. She tried reasoning with him when he railed against his agent, or a new director, calling them all idiots, insisting he deserved more money or better billing. Nothing was good enough for him.

He had long since dropped out of the theater company, and made fun of it, calling them leftover hippies and sixties burnouts. Although he had always despised actors who sold out and considered L.A. the sellout capital, now that he was being pressured by his agents to move there for the film and TV work, his attitude was changing. New York theater, he declared, was dead. Actors who worked for little or nothing were damn fools. New York was where you starved and learned, but L.A. was where you could have a real career.

Margo came home from the theater one night late after a not-so-satisfying performance. She had always been impatient with her own work but lately it had taken a different course. Now she was bored. She would be in the middle of a performance and she would see herself on stage, going through the motions, and think: What am I doing here? Why are all those people sitting there watching me? She was almost tempted to yell "boo!" and ruin the show, break the fragile pact of audience and actors that allowed this pretense.

She wanted to talk to Michael about it because whatever his emotional limitations, he could be smart and objective.

She really didn't expect to find him at home. He'd said he was going out with a couple of his buddies. One of them was leaving for a long location shoot the next day. Margo had told Michael she'd probably go out with the cast for a drink after the show, and she'd be late, too. But she decided at the last minute that she just couldn't bear another night of actor conversation, the endless chatter over who had auditioned for what and if they had a callback and which agents were human.

So she was surprised when she put her key in the upper lock and found it open, but she was glad he was home, because they'd have time to talk.

There was an unfamiliar coat on the chair near the fireplace. And a cigarette with lipstick at the tip in the ashtray they brought out only for guests now, since Michael had quit smoking.

And a murmur of voices coming from the bedroom that she first thought was the television but quickly identified as the unmistakable moans of intense sex.

She stood frozen in the living room for several seconds, then, moved by anger, she went back to the front door, opened it, and closed it, this time hard enough to shake the walls of the apartment.

"Honey, I'm home!" she called out, with exaggerated cheer.

He came rushing out of the bedroom, pulling on a robe.

"Listen, Margo, this crazy thing has happened, uh, my friend Bob, uh, his girlfriend wasn't feeling well, and I said she could come over and, well—"

"Spare me."

The woman came out now. Her only other alternative would have been to go out the window, and they were a little too high up for that. Margo recognized her as the rising young actress with whom Michael had filmed a sexy scene in a new Al Pacino movie a few weeks before.

"It seems to me," said Margo, astonishingly cool, "that in a bedroom farce there should be a back door."

Michael and the woman returned to the bedroom. Margo could hear the murmur of their voices and she wondered if they were making another date to finish what had been so rudely interrupted.

A few minutes later they both emerged. He walked her to the door and kissed her good-bye in the hall. When he came back inside, he said to Margo, "Come on, kiddo, give me a break. It just happened." He talked to her for a long time, apologizing and even, amazingly, making her laugh about the comic aspects of the situation.

But it continued to happen, with different women, over the next months, until the angry scenes turned to hysteria. Margo would rage and cry until Michael slapped her face. He would blame her for provoking him, then they would make up and make love.

When Michael got a serious movie offer, which would keep him in L.A. for three months, he told Margo he had to give up the apartment permanently, that his friend of a friend of the family wanted the place back. She would have to find somewhere else to live because he was moving to L.A.—alone.

Numbly, she got up each morning, and before going to work at the restaurant, she followed up listings in the *Village Voice* and the *New York Times* for available apartments. After three weeks she got lucky. There was a misprint in the paper, listing an apartment on "W. 30th St.," a rent-stabilized two-and-a-half-room walkup for $250 a month. Even in 1979 that was an unusual bargain, and Margo was certain it would be long gone by the time she got there. She happened to be passing the office of the real-estate agent that had listed the apartment, and she stopped in to see if it was still available. Oh, the agent told her peevishly, that was a typo, the apartment was actually on West *Twentieth* Street. Margo was the first one to get to the correct address.

She enrolled in a career-counseling course that cost two hundred dollars and offered a battery of tests and evaluations to help her find her proper career. They determined that she had low salesmanship scores, but high verbal skills, languages, art. She could be an actress, they suggested.

"Thank you," she said, thinking how she could have saved two hundred dollars. "Any other suggestions?"

An editor, perhaps, or something in the social services.

After going back to school for her masters in social work, she was assigned for a year of clinical placement at the sprawling, nineteenth-century-built psychiatric institution at Ward's Island Hospital, where she evaluated individuals, ran groups, and kept copious notes in the patients' files.

She discovered she had a gift for helping people and realized what it was she had found so lacking as an actress. So much of her time had been absorbed by survival jobs and looking for work that she had always felt, on some level, that she was wasting time, taking up space in the world and giving nothing back. Even before homeless people began to pile up on the city streets, she'd wanted to do something, to feel needed. Sometimes she questioned her own dedication, seeing it as just another way to win approval. Saintly Margo, doing good deeds for the poor. She hadn't gone to church since she was a teenager, when she rebelliously rejected her mother's Catholicism, declaring it and all organized religions a load of bunk. Her father, an apathetic Protestant, jokingly called her mother a "Pape" and made fun of "the smoke and magic show" at the Church of Our Lady Queen of Martyrs. Yet Margo found she enjoyed working in the church-run shelters, often side by side with nuns and priests, and sometimes she envied their ascetic, celibate lives.

After Michael, she did not fall in love again for a long time, and when she did, she broke off the relationship when she felt herself getting into another emotional maelstrom. She was too easily distracted by a man, as if her personality disappeared and she became absorbed into his. And she was always attracted to charismatic, complicated, and talented men, which was part of the problem.

She went down the steps to the subway, resigned to a quiet night at home. She would turn on the television and maybe glimpse Michael in a "Rockford Files" rerun or making a minor appearance on some tired new series. His career, while still somewhat active, had never become

the meteoric flight to stardom everyone antici-
pated. Ah, yes, at least life doled out small
amounts of justice, she thought unkindly.

Perhaps tomorrow night Marv DelBello would
prove to be the man of her dreams. Right. And
the people on the streets would awaken in warm
low-rent homes to the sweet, rich aroma of
fresh-baked bread.

3

His apartment was really more of a large closet, although the guy he'd sublet it from was charging enough—you'd think it was a Park Avenue duplex. Art knew it was an illegal sublet and would have been tempted to turn the guy in to his landlord, if he had somewhere else to live.

He had left pieces of his life all over New York City. The whole concept of domestic living defeated him and he drifted from sublet to sublet, six months here, three months there. Either the lease ran out or he did, unable to pay the rent. Before the real-estate boom, it had never been difficult to find cheap places to live in the borderline neighborhoods of Manhattan—someplace where he could give faked references and hand over enough cash to satisfy the landlord or super or subletting tenant—but now even slums were scarce. He was in his fourth apartment in a year and due to leave in six weeks. He'd only taken this one because it included a small, battered upright piano.

He had long ago given up on owning things. There had once been a watercolor painting he'd liked, something he'd bought on impulse when he'd first begun earning money playing the saloons, but he'd left it somewhere, along with countless mugs, socks, watches, cleaning tickets, sheet music, women's phone numbers, furniture, pens, calendars, shoes.

Art stooped down to check out the small refrigerator, unsurprised to find only a beer and an unwrapped, dried old piece of cheese. He stood up and leaned against the wall, weakened by a wave of desolation and self-pity.

Since the end of his last relationship he had become even less organized. The girlfriend had distanced herself, giving him reason upon reason, none of which made any real sense to him, for why it had to end. It had been a slow grind of pain, and now, thinking of doing it again, of loving, if that was what it was, made him weary. How could he ever again muster up that intensity, strip the membrane of unfeeling from his heart or his brain or his cock or wherever it came from?

Women and love and sex baffled him. When he was younger, he'd always tried to be fair and honest with the women he slept with, informing them before bed that he was not likely to become emotionally involved, that he was seeking a night of good sex and little else. They nodded and smiled and slid beneath him and over him and in the morning turned vicious when he kept his word. He had learned not to be so candid.

He wrote his first song the first time he fell in love. His grandparents had decided that summer camp was an integral part of childhood and were also anxious for a child-free summer. The first camp, a rugged sports enclave, was a disaster. Years later, when he read *Lord of the Flies*, he remembered Camp Happy Trails. He was sent home after two weeks for "adjustment problems," but was quickly shipped off to a different sort of camp, the artsy-sensitive Camp Blue Mountain for Music and Art where he blended in with a horde of other adolescent mini-nerds. It was there that he fell in love.

Her name was Cheryl and she was going to be a ballerina. A delicate thirteen, she had slim graceful arms and a young girl's swan neck. She walked like a duck, wore her long brown hair in a severe bun, and carried her things in a sack slung over her shoulder.

Art watched her from afar at first, secretly observing her as she went about her camp life, at the mess hall, at the swimming pool, going to and from dance classes. He could think of no way to attract her attention from her giggling girlfriends or the cuter, older boys she gazed up at with precocious self-assurance. Once in a while she looked his way and smiled, and his day was instantly transformed. One night he performed an impromptu postsupper piano concert. Everyone gathered around while he played Beatles songs, and afterward Cheryl lingered and told him how much she enjoyed his playing. After the others had left the room, he stayed on, writing a love song for Cheryl.

He played it for her the next night, and she kept saying "Oh, how beautiful," which gave him the courage to ask her to accompany him to the next evening's concert. Her acceptance made him delirious and he got permission to go into town so that he could buy her a corsage and a small box of candy, using up his precious allowance.

That night as he sat beside her, the concert a blur of sound and movement, he could not keep himself from touching her. He brushed her shoulder or wrist, took her hand and held it until she drew away to take something out of her bag or fix her hair. At the end of the evening she shook his hand politely, said good night, and went into her cabin. A minute later, as he still stood outside, imagining her kissing the flower gently before setting it into water, he heard instead a shrill burst of laughter from the girls in the cabin.

Over the next days he followed her shamelessly, trying to get a commitment for another date. She'd say things like "Sure!" or "That sounds like fun!" and he'd say "Eight o'clock?" and she'd say "I guess so." And then she wouldn't show up.

"I said I *might* be there," she'd insist the next day.

"No, you said you *would*. I said eight and you said yes, and then you weren't."

"You're so . . . pushy sometimes," she said, shrugging and gazing at him with fawn eyes.

Once he'd heard his mother say, about the bass player's wife, "She just loves him to death," and he'd envisioned the woman, all two hundred pounds of her, rolling onto her husband, kissing him until he suffocated.

After a while, Art became certain that Cheryl was avoiding him. Whenever he went to the places where Cheryl usually was, she wasn't there anymore. And one night, at the evening recital, he saw her holding hands with a long-haired, wiry violist everyone called "Little Duke."

The sensation he felt at that moment was unlike anything he had ever experienced, a deep searing helpless ache.

He wrote Cheryl a letter, neatly block-printed on camp stationery, telling her that they were meant to be together. Around the borders, in tiny print, he copied out the words of the song he had written for her.

Cheryl wrote back, but it was one of her girlfriends who slipped the note into his bunk. He saw the girl coming out. In the note Cheryl said that while he was "very nice," she didn't think of him as a boyfriend but as a "pal."

He went into the bathroom and tore the note

into tiny pieces, flushing them down the toilet. He stared at his stupid face in the mirror for a long time, seeing the distorted features of a monster. He picked up the razor belonging to one of his bunkmates; he had not brought one of his own, having nothing yet to shave. He held it close to his face, closer, imagining blood, imagining Cheryl's tears and regrets.

Cheryl had a favorite jacket, a worn comfortable light brown suede with fringes all along the bottom and shoulders. It had belonged to her older sister, who had gotten it the year Cheryl was born, during the Davy Crockett fad. It was right back in style, as funky hippie chic. Cheryl always wore the jacket on cool evenings and on outings into the woods.

One very hot August night, while the rest of the campers were gathered in the rec hall for the evening's performance—a Gershwin medley by two young classical pianists; an excerpt from *Giselle* danced by Cheryl and several others from the ballet corps; "The Doll Song" from *Tales of Hoffmann,* squeaked out by a somber coloratura—Art slipped away unnoticed by the other campers and their counselors. Once in the hall, he left the building unobserved. It was an especially still night, even the crickets' chorus was subdued in the humidity. A lush summer storm was brewing, one that would bring a deluge of rain but no relief from the moist heat.

He was sweating profusely by the time he got

to the girls' section. He looked carefully in all directions before entering "Bungalow Bar," the cabin Cheryl shared with five other girls and a counselor-in-training.

The suede fringe jacket was hanging on a peg in the corner, next to Cheryl's neatly made upper-bunk bed. He stood still for a moment, distracted by the scent of girls, the labeled trunk at the foot of Cheryl's bed, a box of cookies from home on top. He took a deep breath. Outside, a hoot owl sounded a cool warning and a thrill of fear scurried through him, mixed with excitement.

From his pocket, he withdrew the small double-edged blade he had slipped out of his bunkmate's razor packet and wrapped carefully in a tissue. He seized the jacket, nearly pulling the peg out of the wall in his haste, and brought the edge of the razor up to the first fringe. It was hard going. He had to hold the razor gingerly to keep from cutting himself, even though he had covered one edge with Scotch tape, and the suede was tougher than he'd expected. After the first four fringes, his hand began to ache from the awkward position in which he held it, but one by one the pieces of suede fell to the floor, lying like crushed worms after a rainstorm. He determinedly worked his way along the bottom edge, then started on the shoulders, humming softly to distract himself from the increasing pain in his hand.

A cracking noise like a gunshot sounded. He froze, terrified, and bit his lip. Eyes wide in the dark, he peered out through the screen. The noise had come from the next cabin, the innocently named "Bowl o' Cherries." Someone had gone in, letting the screen door slam shut. Art stood absolutely still until he saw the girl come out again and head back up the hill to the rec hall.

He worked faster now, strip after suede strip fluttering to the wood floor. A strange new energy surged through him. He pressed his hand to his crotch, where his erection swelled in his pants, something that had only happened a few times before and mostly in his sleep. The pressure from the erection seemed to back up against his insides, like it was fighting his body for space. His eyes stung with a mix of pain and pleasure. His hand slipped and he felt the small sting of the razor, saw the drops of blood on the dead suede.

Finished at last, he placed the mutilated jacket back on its peg, leaving the sad, limp fringes where they had fallen.

Later that night, the wail that emerged from Bungalow Bar could be heard all over camp, even in the boys' compound. Lights flashed on like fireflies dotting the hills. The next morning in mess hall an announcement was made about the terrible act of vandalism and how nothing like it had ever happened before at Camp Blue

Mountain for Music and Art. The perpetrator would be caught and punished. If any camper had seen anything out of the ordinary, he or she should report it immediately. Wide-eyed faces stared at one another, each wondering who had been responsible for what soon came to be known as "The Suede Murder."

But nobody had noticed Art leave the rec hall because nobody took much notice of him in general. He almost wanted to be caught, to be able to take credit for his daring deed.

After several days of hollow threats from the staff about punishing everyone, the matter died down. There were the usual tall camp stories of forest demons, Big Foots and ghosts, and some unofficial gossip pointing the finger at a homely, cantankerous dancer who was notoriously jealous of Cheryl, but she had too many alibis to be taken seriously as the Suede Killer.

Art never spoke to Cheryl again and worried a little that she might connect his icy indifference with the death of her jacket, but she did not. He prided himself on the extraordinary effort of will it took to erase her from his mind. It relieved him to know that he could do that, could have such control over his feelings, even if it left a hot coal smoldering in his chest.

When he saw Cheryl glance his way, he repeated over and over to himself, like a mantra: You don't exist, you don't exist. And, after a while, she didn't.

* * *

He played back his messages on the answering machine. The Sally Blaine Agency had called. He used to work for them a lot, taking bookings on cruises where he'd play piano music for Hawaiian-shirted tourists from the suburbs who got drunk before the ship left the harbor. But in the last year he'd been turning the jobs down, preferring to stay in New York where he could make more money playing jobs at the parties of rich people. At the last one he'd told the hostess, a quivery thin woman with thick gold and emeralds ringing a crepey neck, that he'd been born in Singapore, his father a diplomat who died young of a rare jungle disease, and that he could trace his ancestors to the tempestuous Franz Liszt. Whether or not his hosts believed him, they allowed themselves to be charmed, and one job led to another.

He sped the answering machine tape on fast forward, hearing the blur of messages at high speed. Another reminder from the magpie-voiced Sally Blaine of a one-night yacht-party gig tomorrow; a return call from his substitute, Mattie, who confirmed he could take Art's place at Jack's for that evening.

Art cracked open a beer and stood by the window to drink it. There wasn't a lot of furniture in the room. The original tenant didn't have much and neither did Art, so there was a futon and a sling chair, a few wire-carton shelves, and the piano. But there was a nice view of East Fourteenth Street nine flights down. The actor had told Art that subway gunman Bernard Goetz lived a few blocks away, as if that were a selling point. The apartment was in a corner of the building, and when the shades were up, Art could see into the window of the apartment in the opposite corner, where the neighbor's large-screen television was easily visible.

Movement on the screen caught Art's eye. The neighbor's television flashed a group of naked, writhing bodies. Art turned off his lights so as not to be marked a voyeur, and opened the window wide. Peering closer, halfway over the sill, he was disappointed to see that all the bodies were men's, but the activities were vivid and universal enough to stir his interest. Then the film began to fast-forward and Art realized that it was a VCR tape, and the unseen neighbor was hastening through what must be the boring parts. As the speed increased, the sexual groping and thrusting turned into a comic frenzy, like an old silent movie. Body parts passed rapidly before the camera, the participants skittering from one absurd position to another.

Art drew back inside and pulled the window down. He sat on the floor for a while until he had finished his beer. When he finally found the motivation to get up, he checked the window again and saw that his neighbor's television was dark.

4

The cruise to nowhere for Bidden, Latch and Terhune sailed from the West Twenty-third Street Pier on a perfect early-fall evening, the white globe of a full moon hovering overhead. Art was resplendent in a tuxedo, his hair slicked casually back, the suggestion of a five o'clock shadow giving his face rugged mystery. The brandy snifter on the yacht's gleaming white grand piano was filling fast, which gave him great pleasure, just as a special selection of sea songs kept him amused.

Boisterous executives from the recently indicted investment banking firm, whose anniversary party this was, bumped up to the piano with requests for certain songs, some of which he played, some he claimed not to know. Beautiful women were in plentiful supply, but most of them were clinging to the arms of stock analysts and investment bankers.

He was in the middle of Christopher Cross's "Sailing" when the yacht gave a funny lurch, inspiring him to play a few bars of "Oh, They Built the Ship *Titanic*," a ditty he remembered from summer camp long ago. When he glanced up to see if anyone had noticed his musical joke (no one had), he saw a pale blond woman standing across the crowded room watching him intently, an odd expression on her face, a kind of distracted squint. She seemed slightly out of place, not because she was badly dressed—on the contrary, amid the aggressive poufs, bows, and bangles of the late–Christian Lacroix era, she was striking in her simplicity—wearing a short simple blue silk dress that barely concealed the subtle quiver of bare breasts.

She stood very still, a lost statue amid the revelry, her gaze fixed on Art at the piano. He nodded, flashed her a come-hither smile, and turned to the keys for a keenly sensitive arrangement of "Beyond the Sea." When he looked up again, she was taking a glass of champagne from a passing waiter's tray. A man, obviously her date, approached her with two drinks in his hand, saw that she already had one, and laughed. He put his arm around her shoulder and led her out to the deck, where Art lost sight of her.

He was vaguely irritated with her for slipping away, and for dating a man who was clearly a schmuck: too old, too paunchy, too rich, a man who, should Art happen to speak to him, would quickly be questioning him about his "portfolio" and chatting about the condo he'd just turned over; a man whose copy of Donald Trump's *The Art of the Deal* was no doubt dog-eared, with notes in the margins.

A moment later she appeared at the side of the piano, clutching a five-dollar bill in her hand. She had a request, she said. Her voice, he noted immediately, was low and husky, with no trace of an unpleasant regional accent. Too many times he'd spotted an attractive woman, only to be offended when she spoke, her voice coming out in diphthonged New Yorkese, or drawly southern, bimbo voices that made him wonder, should he wake them up in the middle of the night, if they would actually talk that way, or like normal people.

Up close, he saw that she was a natural blonde, the rare cornsilk variety that came with untannable porcelain skin. Although she was not classically beautiful, her eyes a bit too small for perfection, her nose a little long, she had a creamy, radiant sexuality. Deep in his body, in the region of his groin, a small lurch of pleasure nudged him to attention.

But her request, for a recent pop-schlock hit, was a letdown.

"You've got to be kidding," he said, shaking his head.

"You mean you won't play it?"

"Sorry."

"Well, fine, I didn't want to hear it anyway.

He did." She snatched the fiver back from the brandy glass and walked away.

He pounded out a bouncy rendition of "I'm Old-Fashioned," all the while reminding himself of the promise he'd once made, when he started out on the cocktail circuit, that he would not play certain songs. He would not play "Feelings"; he would not play "Tie a Yellow Ribbon Round the Old Oak Tree," or "I've Gotta Be Me," or "The Greatest Love of All"; by no means would he ever play "Don't Cry Out Loud."

On his break he went out onto the deck and leaned on the railing, watching the water foam up against the side of the boat. The scent of the air, the wind hard on his face, blew back an old memory. He'd been twenty-four when he'd spent six months playing piano on a world cruise on a huge ocean liner. He'd lived first-class, wearing a tux every night, smiling for the rich-rich, a young, handsome, toy-boy with talent and time on his hands for bored, aging wives, bored young wives. The French female singer who headlined the entertainment wanted him all to herself and hurled his things around the stateroom when he clumsily tried to break free, and she left the cruise early.

As they sailed into each new, foreign port, he felt a surge of anticipation, as if here he would find what he was seeking. And when they sailed out again, his suitcase stuffed with new postcards he never sent, souvenirs he'd lost along the way, he knew he had not found it.

He made friends with the English singer who replaced the French chanteuse. She was traveling with her boyfriend, who claimed to be a rock guitarist but never played in Art's presence. He was punkish and skinny and irritating, but he had a boundless supply of good dope. After a while, Art got over his vague itchy desire for the English singer and the nagging hope that her raggy, wasted "chap" would drop overboard. The three of them got into the habit of staying up until dawn every night, wandering the ship from the Diamond Ballroom to the Pirates' Cove Lounge, lying about in either Art's stateroom or his friends'.

One night they explored further.

Stoned and giddy, they found their way up to the very top outside deck. Scaling a narrow ladder, they climbed to the base of one of the two giant smokestacks perched high atop the ship. It was surrounded by a low fence which they climbed over easily. Far below, the black midwinter Atlantic Ocean thrashed; they were as far from land as anyone could be. The wind blew so fiercely they could not hear anything but its roar. It seized their shouted words and hurled them out into the night. The ship dipped and plunged ahead through the sea's convulsions, and the waves seemed to be reaching up with grasping foamy fingers to the three small people who balanced precariously above.

Art was the first to discover that he could actually lean back against the wind and it would hold him up, suspended in space. His hair, much longer then, whipped into his eyes, his tux jacket twisted madly around his chest. He let out a scream of pure pleasure and terror, the sound instantly borne away into the night. Through tearing eyes he glimpsed the faces of his companions, their heads leaning back, mouths open, demonically possessed by the wind that held them in suspended animation.

How simple it would be to fly, he thought, to let himself be carried off on the talons of the wind. Perhaps he had been meant to die that night, to be blown screaming into the sea. Or maybe he should have followed his impulse to give the raggy chap a quiet shove into oblivion.

"Thinking of jumping?" said a quiet voice behind him. He started, opening his eyes. For a second he was not sure where he was, but a glimpse of the Statue of Liberty glowing on the horizon brought him back. The blond woman in the blue dress was standing behind him.

"Looks like a pretty good night for a swim," he managed to retort, stepping away from the rail.

"Why wouldn't you play the song I wanted? Isn't that your job?"

"No. Not really. What if you wanted 'The Flight of the Bumblebee'?" He was noticing the scent of her perfume, musky and deep. He reached out to catch a passing waiter and took a glass of champagne.

"I hate this stuff," he said, drinking it down in one swallow. He nudged a cigarette out of his pack and lit up. She waved at the smoke that came her way.

"I know," he said, "terrible habit. Someday I'll quit. But not now."

"I quit."

"Good for you. What do you do for fun?"

She looked up at him, raised one eyebrow slightly, and smiled, her gray eyes playful. "Actually, I'm thinking of getting a pet. Something different. Like an iguana. Or a ferret. Something mean."

"Why is that?"

She shrugged. "Just the kind of gal I am."

"Mean?"

"No." She flushed slightly. "Not really."

"Remember those little turtles everyone used to have?" he asked. "No, you're probably too young—"

"Puh-leeze, I'm older than you are, I bet."

"How old?"

"How old are you?" she persisted.

"Thirty," he lied for no particular reason. It just came out.

"See? I'm thirty-seven."

"You don't look it."

"Well, as Gloria Steinem said, sort of: this is what thirty-seven looks like."

"Oh. It looks good."

"Thank you, but what else could you say? 'Yes, you look your age, no actually, you look older'? It's such a line, like nowadays men always have to tell you how smart you are: 'I've never gone out with a woman of your intelligence before. It's so refreshing.' Ha! Refresh *this!*"

"You're very intelligent. It's so refreshing."

She laughed and he liked the way her eyes crinkled up at the corners and nearly disappeared. She had straight, very white teeth that appeared to be natural. He imagined her stretched out beneath him, her sleek pale body nude, maybe bound lightly with scarves, her eyes shut, her mouth opened and moaning.

"Anyway," she was saying, "I *do* remember those turtles. People always brought them back from Florida—"

"And they had palm trees painted on their backs—"

"And they always died."

"What ever happened to them?" he mused.

"I guess they don't make them anymore."

"What do you mean 'make them'? They're hatched, not factory-made."

"Maybe they're extinct," she said with a shrug.

"That's impossible, they were all over the place. Like pigeons. It would be like pigeons becoming extinct."

"I don't know. Maybe they just stopped painting them. I think it was supposed to be cruel or something. It made their shells go soft and then they died and got thrown in the toilet."

"I see you're an animal lover."

"I didn't mean *I* threw them in the toilet. *People* did. To feed the alligators." She laughed sharply. "Anyway, they're not animals, they're crustaceans."

A group of partyers had come out onto the deck, crowding Art and the woman. They stepped into the main hall, raising their voices to be heard over the music and the noise. Two men nearby were talking loudly about lawn equipment. A disparate chorus of invisible watches beeped the half hour.

"So, what *is* your favorite song?" he asked her. "Don't you have a request?"

She closed her eyes, thinking, then looked straight at him. "I really love 'Bewitched, Bothered and Bewildered.' "

He had the peculiar sensation that all movement stopped around him, bringing into crystal focus the slight gesture of her hand up to her lips. As if this moment was where he had been heading for a long, long time. He wondered if she felt it, too.

"Oh, there's my date," she said without enthusiasm.

Real life was restored. Art saw the paunchy guy waving at her over the heads of several people.

"I don't think they're crustaceans at all," Art

said, picking up the thread of their conversation. "I think they're in the seal family."

"Are you kidding? Lobsters and crabs are their brothers and sisters."

"Then I guess they're Crustacean-Americans," he remarked.

The date reached them. "So there you are!" he said, glancing at Art and anticipating an introduction.

After a slight pause she said, "This is the piano player."

"Art Glenn," the piano player added.

"And this is Marv DelBello," she said. The two men shook hands awkwardly. Marv's was damp and slightly greasy from hors d'oeuvres.

"And you are?" Art asked the woman.

"Oh, you two don't know each other?" said Marv. "It seemed like you did."

"Margo Magill," she said, offering her hand. She smiled slightly when he took it, a blink of significance and instant connection in her eyes.

"Is that a stage name?" he asked.

"No. Just my mother's talent for alliteration. If I'd been a boy, I'd have been Mickey." She pulled away the hand Art was still holding.

He turned to Marv. "What are turtles?"

"Little round things with hard shells."

"No, I mean, what family are they from?"

Margo interrupted. "Oh, very *good* families!"

"I mean species, what animal family, you know, crustaceans, seals, what?"

Marv's brow creased. "Reptiles."

"No!" Art and Margo said in unison. "Are you sure?" she added.

"Definitely. I'm really good at Trivial Pursuit." Marv took Margo's arm possessively. "It was nice meeting you, uh, Arthur."

"Nice meeting you, too, Marv. Margo." He looked at her but her face was impassive. "I have to do my next set."

"Say," said Marv, "Could you play 'Don't Cry Out Loud'?"

"No, I don't think so." He walked away.

> ". . . somewhere, beyond the sea
> somewhere, waiting for me . . ."

The yacht docked quietly at the Twenty-third Street Pier, the city looming, dense and real the way he loved and dreaded it. He hadn't had a chance to talk to Margo again and he glimpsed her leaving the boat with her date. He closed the cover over the piano keys, gathered his music, and went in search of the person who was holding his check.

5

Art maneuvered his way through a line of actors crowding the narrow hallway of the aged rehearsal studio and entered Studio 3A. The last thing he wanted to do this early morning, other than get up at all, was to play auditions for a parade of singers.

Gerry Skinner, the director, was seated behind a long table in the mirror-lined room. He was pale and thin, his hair much grayer than it had been the last time Art saw him, and he wore a long white silk aviator's scarf wrapped around his neck. He'd been the director of the "Broadway on Board" cruises Art had played. Despite his gaunt appearance, he greeted Art with a lot of manic energy for that hour of the morning, and introduced him to the others at the table.

"Artie was our music director for 'Broadway Bored,'" Gerry remarked. "We both earned sainthood for all those Jerry Herman medleys, but Art was *salvation*. And he's a *dynamite* composer! What ever became of that show you were writing? With that song I liked so much?"

"Not a lot. It had a showcase."

"The music was divine!" Gerry enthused.

Feeling slightly queasy, Art shook hands around the table. The young producer rose to his full five feet three inches and seized Art's hand, offering unsolicited information about his background, particularly the Yale Drama School. The composer was a sallow woman in her early forties with a damp palm who narrowed her eyes at Art with an expression of "we're both serious artists." Next to her was the lyricist/book writer, a slim eager young man, wearing a small gold hoop in one ear.

Art sat at the piano and played a few chords, working the stiffness out of his fingers. The instrument was cheap but at least it was in tune. He sipped hot coffee from a Styrofoam cup, anxiety gnawing in his belly, triggered by the reminder of his songs and the failed show.

"Send in the first victim!" called Gerry.

A plump young woman, the stage manager, led in a pretty actress with short blond hair.

"Hi, everybody! I like to be first when everyone's still fresh!" she said jovially, using some ice-breaking technique she'd probably picked up in an overpriced "how to audition" class. There was a beat of silence.

"So, what are you going to sing for us?" asked Gerry.

"'Memories.' From *Cats.*" She placed the sheet music in front of Art. He dutifully began the opening chords. She looked at him several times before she began, as if she were sending him a telepathic message. He played the intro again and this time she began singing in a high reedy soprano that occasionally found the pitch. After sixteen bars Gerry called out a cheerful "Thank you!"

The young woman left the room and a perky young man took her place.

"What are you going to sing for us?" asked Gerry.

"Well, I wasn't sure if you wanted a ballad or an up tune, so I brought—"

"Just sing what you feel most comfortable with."

"Okay. I guess, 'On the Street Where You Live.'" He handed it to Art. "Could you play it a third lower?" Art began the song, struggling with the transposition, which wasn't his forte. The singer stopped. "Uh, sorry, but a little faster, with kind of a fastish feel?" Art resumed in a driving tempo.

Gerry sang out, "Thank you!"

The singer paused. "Do you want to hear my up tune?"

"No, I think we've heard all we need. Very nice. Could you send in the next one?"

* * *

On the break, Art bummed a cigarette from the composer, stood in a corner taking in the smoke, and gazed out the window at the far end of the rehearsal room into a back alley between Forty-sixth and Forty-seventh Streets. In a rear window of the hotel across the way, a black maid was moving back and forth, making the bed. He could almost feel the cool anonymous sheets of a hotel bed, all the interchangeable, forgettable places he had stayed in his life.

He scanned the other windows of the hotel, seeking signs of movement, but the shades were drawn or the windows too high. His own reflection in the glass glinted back, the white of his cotton sweater, the wave of maple-brown hair catching the light. He sucked hard on the cigarette, letting its pleasant poison fill him.

"Artie," called the director, "we're starting again!"

The stage manager ushered in the next auditioner.

Art started to stand up as soon as he saw her, started to say that they'd already met, but stopped himself in time. It was the pale hair that deceived him, and her profile, and the blue dress. The combination formed a different image, one that was already on his mind. But this woman was a stranger, not Margo from the party at all. He watched her carefully, picking out the differences. This woman was actually prettier in an actressy way.

She smiled brilliantly at him as she handed

over her music. Charm the accompanist. Well, it worked; he was easy. He played her song with extra care, a long, mournful ballad. She sang well and Gerry promised her a callback. The actress left in a swirl of happiness.

On the next break he found the ancient phone booth and ran his fingernails idly over the bumpy patterned brown walls inside, causing a tickling sensation in his arms.

"Directory assistance."

"I need the name of a business called Bidden, Latch, something, something, and something, I can't remember the rest."

"That's Bidden with a *B* and two *D*'s, Latch, Sumthin with an *S*—"

"No! I mean, yes, Bidden with a *B* and two *D*'s, but the rest of the name—"

Suddenly the operator clicked off and a computer was giving him the number, the artificial voice rising and falling in arbitrary cadence. Repeating the number to himself, he dropped in a quarter and dialed.

"Bidden, Latch and Terhune, please hold."

The McDonald's jingle played in his ear. A waiting actor rapped sharply on the phone-booth door and looked questioningly at Art. He shook his head and turned away, clutching the phone. The operator finally came back on the line.

"Margo Magill, please." After a pause he was informed that there was no one at the firm by that name.

"Okay, what about, what was his name, Marv . . . DelBello?"

"I'll check, please hold."

A buzz, a click, a ring.

"Accounting. DelBello."

"Oh. Uh, hi. You don't really know me. I was the piano player on the cruise party for the . . . your company the other night, we spoke briefly. Now I know this is going to sound a little weird, but the young lady you were with, Margo Magill, well, she was interested in me playing a party? But in the rush I forgot to give her my card and I don't have her number, so I was wondering if, uh, you could, give me her number where she works or if I could leave a message?"

After a pause the accountant said, "She was my *date*. You want me to give out my *date's* phone number? I don't know you from Adam. You wouldn't even play my request."

"Well, this is just business, it's just work, you know? I'm not looking to marry her—"

"I'm not seeing her anymore."

"Oh."

"It wasn't any big thing to begin with. I thought maybe we could have a good time. I see her every month or so when I do the books at the hospital and I thought we could have a good time, but I'll tell you honestly, she was real uptight the whole evening."

"I see. The hospital. That's Lenox Hill, right?"

"No, Bellevue."

"Of course. Bellevue. She told me that. I

should have remembered and called her there, I have this sick friend in Lenox Hill, so it's kind of on my mind. Sorry to have bothered you. What department was she in?"

"Psychiatric. She's some kind of social worker. Works with flakes all day long. Must rub off."

"Thanks a lot, Marv."

"Any time you need an accountant, I work free-lance outside the company. Good rates."

"Sure."

"Hope your friend gets better."

"Who?"

"The one in Lenox Hill."

"Oh, right. He's fine. He's dead. Well, not dead exactly and not really fine, he's . . . in a coma, but they expect a full recovery."

He put down the receiver and rubbed his hand over his face. When he opened his eyes, he saw Gerry's features pressed against the glass, squashed and distorted. Startled, he got up too fast and bumped his head on the booth's low ceiling. Gerry drew back, his face restored, beckoning silently on the other side of the glass.

6

The digital clock on top of the building across the street told her that the temperature was eighty-nine degrees, the time 6:24. Between the heat and the boredom, she was getting a headache.

Eighty-nine. Six-twenty-four. Eighty-nine. Six-twenty-five.

Susan had only been standing outside for an hour and it already felt like a day in hell. Her arm ached from holding out fliers to the swarms exiting the subway station at Seventy-second Street and Broadway. Hordes of them squeezed through the small doors and expanded into the streets like an overflowing toilet. Stopping at the gourmet shops for their cute little microwave dinners, and at the video stores for tonight's movie, and disappearing into ritzy co-ops.

"Check it out," she said softly, ignored unless she pushed the flier right up into their faces. Then all she'd get was a wave of the hand, like they were chasing away an insect, or maybe, just maybe, one of them would deign to actually take a flier and look at it before stuffing it into the nearest trash can or letting it drop like a dirty tissue onto the sidewalk.

She walked past the newsstand outside the subway station, to the corner, counting her steps: One. Two. Three. Four. It was important to pause on an even number. She stopped at the curb. Waiting for the light to change, she felt someone brush up against her and she turned, glaring The Look at the person, who didn't meet her eyes. Of course not. They were afraid of The Look.

As she crossed the street, she counted again, making sure that all her strides were even. She reached the Papaya store corner, waited, and crossed Seventy-second Street, arriving in exactly seventeen steps, which was not a good omen, so she backtracked and recounted to eighteen.

She leaned the heavy plastic bag, filled with the evening's supply of fliers, against the wall of the bank, took a big handful, and planted herself in the middle of the sidewalk. A few yards away, a shabbily dressed man was holding the bank's door open for the people who went in and out, shaking a cardboard cup at them for tips. Susan was disgusted at how many gave him money, like they owed him something for opening the door when they were perfectly capable of doing it themselves.

They didn't hear him mutter curses at them under his breath when they walked away without giving him money, or see him meet his pals later, high-fiving and smoking crack in the doorway around the corner.

She saw her reflection in the bank's window and noticed that she had a light around her. Boyd had told her it was her aura but he'd been high at the time and he was full of shit even when he wasn't using. But then she'd read in the *Star* that human beings all have auras, and in some people, the special ones, it really glows. Like a firefly at night.

Susan knew that she was more than special. She had powers she hadn't even begun to use. Like The Look, which she used only a small part of, so as not to burn people up on the spot.

"Check it out. Clancy's Bar and Grill. Great food. Cheap prices." She stepped forward to hand a flier to a young woman, who actuallly veered away to avoid her.

What would it hurt to take the goddamn flier? That was what she never understood, the way they acted like she was offering them shit on a stick.

A man walked by and Susan stuck out her hand. He took the thing and threw it on the ground without even looking at it. Litter pig. People really made her sick.

She tried again, as a woman in a business suit and sneakers passed. The woman actually smiled and took the flier.

Like she felt sorry for her or something. Well, don't do me any fucking favors, bitch.

What did it matter? She wasn't getting paid per flier anyway, just for each hour. Long, leg-tiring hours.

It was time for a cigarette break.

She leaned against the bank window and lit up with a pack of matches from Jack's Café-Bar, Amsterdam Avenue. Now that was a classy place, the kind where she belonged. And as soon as she got her modeling career off the ground, when she walked into a place like that, everybody would turn around, asking who she was, instead of acting like they didn't even see her.

She reached into the small purse that hung across her shoulder so that no one could yank it away from her, and took out her round mirror, blurry with powder, and stared at her face. There was just the beginning of a line between her eyes and she felt a jolt of panic. She could not get lines. If she got lines and wrinkles, she would never be famous.

Her face looked strange to her today. Each feature seemed disconnected from the other, like one of those weird old paintings people called "modern" even though they were painted like a hundred years ago.

The red mark was still on her cheek from where Boyd had hit her again. With the ointment the drugstore guy had given her, she carefully massaged the spot, over and over. She also rubbed it on the faint wrinkle, methodically trying to erase it.

She wondered if Boyd was surprised when he woke up and found her gone. She'd taken a few of his pathetic things and thrown them in the garbage while he was out cold and she grinned to think of him racing around the room, sweating from withdrawal and looking for his paraphernalia. He'd always tried to get her to do all that shit, but she told him she had her career to think about. Sure, she'd snort coke whenever he got some, but she sure wasn't going to smoke any crack or stick needles in her skin. Boyd thought that was really funny.

She would have liked to do some more damage to him and his stuff but she was just glad to be out of there, out of his crummy room. He'd never find her now. She knew how to make herself invisible. That had been over a week ago and she'd heard on the street that he'd been busted. She hoped that he was getting reamed up the ass in prison right that very moment.

She'd slept on the subway for a couple of days, then at a women's shelter, but that place was the pits, with all kinds of dumb rules and loonies running around. If she stayed there, she'd be mental in no time. Now Clancy was letting her crash in the back room of the bar, as long as she gave out his fliers all fucking night. Like his rotten food and a cot in the back was worth her time.

With a deep sigh, she crushed out her cigarette on the ground and picked up the fliers again.

Seven-ten. Eighty-eight degrees. At least it was getting cooler.

She felt a little better.

Susan Starlight. Susan Surprise. Susan Suzanne. Those were all good stage names. Maybe a rock star. She could write those songs and wear fancy rock-goddess underwear and dance around. She started doing it right there, playing a mind tape of "Respect Yourself" and dancing. People were looking at her and she knew they were thinking that she was an undiscovered talent and wondering why she was forced to dole out leaflets on the street instead of starring on MTV.

Jump, twist. Jump, twist, turn her head from side to side. The sweat rolled down her back under her thin blouse, but she didn't care. Her unevenly chopped hair hung lank over her forehead, trickling into her eyes. She was joyous, perfect, magical. A woman passed by wheeling a young child in a stroller. The baby pointed at Susan and laughed. Susan pointed back. The mother pushed the stroller faster. Susan had plenty of room on the sidewalk now. Everyone had made way for her, recognizing her magic. She danced on, pretending to be a robot, a bunny, a pony, dancing and dancing to the music that spiraled and whirled within her head like a meteor shower.

7

"They took my songs, you know? Stole 'em right out while I was sleeping. Pulled 'em out of my brain. They can do that."

Margo nodded understandingly as the woman continued, speaking in a drawl that recalled hippie slang and the Texas prairie.

"And they had all their gases ready, they carry them in Tums packs, you know? They were going to slip the gases into my guitar, poison me through my music, you get me?" She tapped at the battered guitar case on the floor, plastered with old travel stickers and secured with ropes that looped and looped around it, so that it would take a person at least a half an hour to liberate the instrument, if there was actually one inside.

"Have you been taking your medication, Emma?" Margo asked.

The woman lowered her voice to a whisper.

"I'm not called Emma now. They're after my soul, you know? So I gotta fool 'em."

"What are you called?"

"That's secret." Emma looked long and meaningfully into Margo's eyes. "But I can tell I can trust you. Vibrations, you know? Ginseng."

"What?"

"Ginseng. That's my name now."

"Ah." Margo glanced surreptitiously at her watch: 9:20. She had been at the shelter since six and there were still at least a dozen women waiting to see her, sitting on chairs, pacing around, drinking stale coffee from the huge stained metal urn. A layer of smoke from many cigarettes formed a veil beneath the low ceiling. The waiting women chatted among themselves. Or to themselves. Voices and whispers bouncing off the dingy, utility-green walls of the shelter, a converted church basement. Beds were lined up along one wall. Margo visited one afternoon a week, along with a nurse, to evaluate the women and recommend treatments for their myriad physical and mental ills.

She'd hoped to get out by nine, go home, and shower and change before meeting Art Glenn at the club where he played piano, but now it looked as if she wouldn't get out until after eleven. And by then she'd probably be too tired to go out. On the other hand, whenever she thought about the cute piano player, she got a little charge of adrenaline, a tantalizing stir she hadn't felt in a long time.

"It's important that you take your pills, Em—Ginseng. That way we can help you get a place to live. But I see here—" She looked down at the notes prepared by the head of the shelter, an energetic and dedicated nun. "I see that you were asked to leave Friday night because you were causing trouble." The actual words in the report were: "Emma Lee Sands hostile and disruptive, accused another lady of trying to poison her while she slept, started a fight in the shower area, night volunteer called police, who evicted Emma."

"That's what I'm trying to tell you!" the woman shrieked, causing the ones who were lying on their cots hoping for some early sleep to look up. A voice called out hoarsely, "Keep it down! Can't a person get some goddamned quiet?"

Emma/Ginseng continued, in a stage whisper, "She was getting into my brain, you know what that's like, right?" As she went on to describe the conspiracies against her, Margo studied her. She must have been really pretty once, but now her hair was badly cropped and bleached, the roots half grown out, deep lines etched in her face. According to the records, she was forty-three, although she looked nearly ten years older. But she still had beautiful light blue eyes and a slim attractive body. Maybe she really had been a musician once. The first time Margo met her, Emma had described in detail her travels with a rock band, but whether she'd actually

played or just followed a boyfriend was any-
body's guess. She'd lived in San Francisco in
the flower-child era and Margo could well imagine her, a lissome long-haired beauty, playing
her music on the street, indulging in the fad
drugs of the era, and living on love. And if one
day someone had approached her and said, "In
twenty years you will be old before your time,
paranoid, and living on the New York City
streets," she would have laughed, taken another toke, and strummed a few more choruses
of "Light My Fire."

"Do you still have your medication?"

"I lost 'em," she said evasively. Margo knew
she had probably sold the pills. Some speed
freak or barbiturate addict had gotten an unpleasant surprise when the antidepressants
provided no high.

"Well, you know I can't write a prescription,
but take this note to the clinic." Margo scrib-
bled out her recommendation that Emma be is-
sued more of the same medication. "You know
where the clinic is?"

"Sure. I was there for a week," she said
proudly. "They know me." Emma picked up her
guitar case and shambled away, the ropes
around the case dangling and dragging on the
ground. Margo checked her list.

"Sister Rose!" she called out.

An elderly black woman approached, pushing
a small shopping cart filled with swollen Hefty
bags and decorated with hand-drawn signs that

said "The Lord Loves You!", "Sister Rose Knows!", "Jesus Forgives and Gives, Too!" She wore a beanie hat with a yellow pinwheel on cop.

"Good day, doctor! Or should I say good night!" Sister Rose said cheerfully. Margo refrained from correcting her once again that she was not a doctor, just a lowly social worker. Sister Rose had roamed the city for years. No one at the shelter had been able to track down any of her family, although she sometimes spoke of a daughter and a dead husband. "Have you heard the Good News today?"

"Yes, Sister Rose, I have. Did you want to see me about something in particular?" Surely she had not waited two hours on a metal chair to inform Margo that Jesus was her Personal Savior? On the other hand, if the woman weren't sitting here, she'd probably be sitting in the bus terminal or preaching herself hoarse near Times Square.

"I've got a pain in my heart—right here." Sister Rose was pointing to her chest. "It goes on and on all day and I been to see the nurse lady and she send me to the clinic doctor and he listen and he say he don't hear nothin' and maybe it be in my head? An' I say, no sir, it in my heart!"

"Have you been sleeping indoors? The nights are getting chillier, you have to take care of yourself."

"Jesus take care of Sister Rose, I got nothin'

to fear when Jesus is near. But I ain't been getting my checks, doctor. Sister Luke say they ain't been none come here and I'm suppose to call this numbuh, but I done get nothin' 'cep a busy signal."

"I'll call HRA tomorrow, but we have to be able to reach you. I see you haven't been here in a month."

"I don't like the shelter, too many crazy women!" Sister Rose crinkled up her dark face in disgust. "They got no decency, no manners. They take crack. And"—she lowered her voice conspiratorially—"they let mens in in the middle of the night. I woke up to find a man over my bed."

"That must have been one of the volunteers. No other men come in here and the doors are locked."

"Wasn't no volunteer. Every night they lets the mens in." Sister Rose's lips tightened and Margo knew there was no point in trying to argue with her.

This was one of those nights when she ended up feeling beaten down and defeated by the endless parade of problems. If she went home, she'd wind up lying in the dark hearing their voices in her head, their sad stories of bad luck and abusive men and drinking and drugs and troubles. She would be overwhelmed by their stupidities, their inability to plan ahead, to take charge of their lives. She would get angry, thinking: What's the point of even trying to help? Maybe she was getting too old to keep up the facade of optimism in a city that was increasingly overwhelmed by poverty. Why didn't she just move out, go somewhere clean and new. But where?

If someone had come up to her twenty years ago, when she was an ingenuous seventeen, and whispered, "You will be unmarried, childless, and barely making a living as a social worker," she would have laughed, taken another toke, and sung a few more choruses of "Fire and Rain."

It was getting late, and there were still so many. Sister Rose pushed her cart down the aisle. The shelter's beds were filled to capacity and there was not room in the inn for her that night.

I deserve to go out later, Margo resolved as the next client shambled toward her desk. She got up and poured a cup of coffee from the battered old tureen. Taking a sip of the stale bitter liquid, she began her next interview, energized by the horrible coffee and the vague hope that maybe something wonderful might happen that night.

8

All night long Art waited for Margo to show up at Jack's. He'd called her, tracked her down with some difficulty, feeling like a fool when he got Bellevue Hospital on the line, not even knowing what she did there. But after a succession of impatient transfers, he finally got her on the phone. She was a psychiatric social worker, she told him, and her specialty was the homeless. She was one of those people who rode around in a van at night rescuing freezing crazies in the winter, ever since the mayor had decided it was a good idea to get them off the streets.

She remembered Art, all right, and she seemed to enjoy the fact that he'd gone to some trouble to find her. Nobody goes to the trouble anymore, she said. If it isn't easy, they don't bother. She told him that she worked most nights, too, but promised to stop by Jack's after her shift. If *he* promised to play her requests this time.

Anything, he assured her.

You know, she said, you're just the kind of man I should stay away from.

How does she know that so soon? he wondered, and was about to say something but she'd already hung up the phone, leaving him unsettled.

He segued from "Love Walked In" to "The Lady Is a Tramp." After the set he sat at the bar and listened to Jack's mournful tale of losing a bundle on the horses that day. Art could not sympathize with people who gambled and then griped about losing, as if it were a surprise, as if everyone were supposed to win.

"You're the piano player." A woman slid onto the stool next to him. She was not Margo Magill in any way. This woman's eyes were reddened, like a Visine "before" commercial. Her dark hair was cut short in the front, longer in the back, trailing into a wispy tail. The front had been spiked up but had succumbed to gravity and fell over her forehead in limp strands. She rummaged in a soiled plastic bag and pulled out a stack of leaflets, setting them upside down on the bar. Art craned his neck to read: "Grand Opening! Clancy's Bar and Grill! Old-Fashion Prices!"

"I been giving these out all fucking night and

my feet are killing me," she announced to anyone who might be listening.

She took off one of her high heels and rubbed
a callused bare foot. "I know, I should wear low
shoes, but my legs look too stumpy."

"They look fine to me," he offered.

"Oh, yeah? Thanks."

She dug in her purse some more and removed
a tube of ointment, squeezed a dot on her finger, and dabbed it onto a small red spot on her
cheek. The spot grew fiery as she rubbed at it.

"I was gonna be a model but look at this! Girl
attacked me on the street when I was givin' out
these fuckin' fliers. She scratched my face. She
coulda gave me AIDS, you know. The doctor
said it would be okay if I rubbed this stuff on
four times a day, so I do it eight times. I figure
it'll get better faster, right? 'Cause I don't want
nothin' happening to my face. That's my fuckin'
future. Like that girl, that model? Got her face
all slashed up by a guy? People are fuckin'
crazy. But she's doin' all right, she gets herself
in all the magazines and she went on TV with
her slashed-up face and suddenly she's a star.
Some people got all the luck."

Art eased himself off the stool.

"I come in here a lot, Jack lets me rest at the
bar, sometimes he buys me a drink."

"What would you like?"

"Rye and ginger ale. That's the only thing I
like to drink."

He nodded at Jack, who brought one over.

"This girl that attacked me, can you believe it?"

"Why did she—"

" 'Cause she was fuckin' crazy, that's why. She bumps into me, on purpose, you know." She looked at him meaningfully. "So I call her a dirty whore and she knocks me down, comes at my face. I hate this job. This is the only thing in my whole job that I enjoy, coming in here for a drink and sitting down. Other than that, I hate every minute of my life."

"Why don't you try some other kind of job?"

"My husband's out of work," she replied, by way of explanation.

"What does he do?"

She shifted on the stool, gulped down her drink. She wasn't unattractive, her features were even enough, but there was no curiosity in her eyes, and her mouth had a tight dry set to it.

"Nothin', absolutely nothin'. He watches TV all day, when he's *supposed* to be takin' care of *my* kid."

"I meant what kind of job does he do when he *is* working?"

"Oh. He paints bridges."

Art entertained himself by picturing a man in a torn T-shirt, holding a beer in one hand and a paintbrush in the other, standing in front of an easel, laboriously copying the Brooklyn Bridge.

"I come in nearly every night and I sit over here, but you never see me, I guess. I like the way you play and you sing good, too." She leaned close to him and he could smell perspiration mixed with faded cheap perfume. "Do you have any blow?"

He shook his head.

"Shit. I could use a little, just to get through the rest of the night. I gotta give out these stupid things till midnight. I mean, who gives a fuck, I could dump the whole mess in the garbage, who would know? I mean, who cares about these fliers. There's nobody out there but bag ladies and sleaze buckets. You sure you don't have any blow? Or you know where I can get some?"

Ignoring her, he waved for another Jack Daniel's. His watch said 12:20, and it didn't look like Margo would be showing up. For an instant he could taste the sharp pleasure of cocaine at the back of his throat, the inevitable lift. If he had some, and Margo came, he'd be better company. If she didn't, at least he'd have a way of feeling good.

The woman leaned in again. "Listen, I'll make it worth your while. . . ."

He was about to say yes, to make the necessary phone call to the dealer who supplied Jack's cokehead yuppies, when he saw her come through the door.

Margo didn't see him at first. She looked toward the piano in the corner, then peered around the room until she spotted Art at the bar. He wished he could have been playing for her entrance so that he could appear artistically distracted, instead of sitting with the flier girl. He watched Margo cross the room to him.

"So you made it."

"I made it. Things were crazy down there."

"That must've been a surprise."

"I mean hectic."

She removed her aviator-style brown jacket, revealing a pale blue cotton sweater over tight dark brown slacks.

"I didn't have time to dress up or anything," she apologized.

"You look gorgeous. You would look gorgeous in a grocery bag."

"I have a whole wardrobe of grocery bags."

Just then the flier girl piped up, "Can you do 'Don't Cry Out Loud'?"

"No."

"You're kidding. Everybody knows that one."

Margo and Art looked at each other and burst out laughing.

"What's so funny?" she asked, gathering her fliers and putting on her coat.

"Nothing," Art replied, gazing at Margo. The girl was like a shadow moving about in the background. After a while she left.

"I guess we weren't very nice," said Margo.

"No," he agreed. "But I was distracted."

"Oh, yes?"

"Oh, yes."

Jack interrupted. "Artie! Music!"

"I'll be back," he assured her.

"I thought you might be."

"Any requests?"

"Ha! As if you'd listen."

Discarding his alphabetized system, he played "Bewitched, Bothered and Bewildered," which was very much the way he felt. Knowing she was watching inspired him.

"I don't usually do this," she said as they climbed the three flights to her apartment. Outside her door were four Chinese takeout menus. She leaned down to pick them up. "Invite men home on the first date, that is."

"Neither do I. Listen, this may be important, but do you always get so many menus?"

Margo put her key in the door. "As a matter of fact this is nothing. The record is eight in one day. The funny thing is, I never, ever see anyone distributing them. They just appear. I think they're beamed over from the one huge, underground Chinese restaurant. There's only one, you know."

"Oh, I knew that. It's the same with the Indian restaurants downtown."

She laughed and opened the door.

Her apartment was small and warm, in temperature as well as ambience, two adjoining rooms with windows facing West Twentieth Street, covered with slightly faded deep blue curtains that almost matched a shaggy rya rug. There was a large map covering one wall, the kind that usually hung in school classrooms, and several posters from theatrical productions. A desk in the corner was piled high with papers, files, letters, magazine articles. He idly picked up the top one, a journal with a cover article on the mentally ill homeless. Although the apartment was messy, it had what his lacked: a sense of belonging.

"Would you like a drink?"

"What have you got?"

She opened the refrigerator. "Light beer, wine, and wine."

"No whiskey?"

"Sorry."

"Beer, I guess. Do you mind if I smoke?"

"Yes, but go ahead."

"I'll sit by the window."

She turned on some music, a cassette of some lulling, sensual New Age guitarist.

"You don't mind the audio-Valium, do you?" she asked.

"No, I like it." He finished his cigarette and crushed it out on the sill, pushing the butt out and closing the window.

"Come here."

She was standing by the divider between the living room and the kitchen, holding two glasses of beer. He crossed to her.

"I hope you don't mind the taste of a smoker," he said. "Because I'm going to kiss you."

"I don't mind," she said, barely audible.

He took the glasses out of her hand and set them on the counter. He touched her hair lightly and leaned down to her, just brushing her lips. Her eyelids fluttered closed and she let out a small moan. He ran his forefinger along the outline of her mouth, opening it slightly, then kissed her again, tasting her. Powerful sensations surged up inside him. He ran his hand over her breasts, bare beneath her sweater. The kiss went on a long time.

"Well," she said, catching her breath and giving a nervous laugh. "Is, um, this where we're supposed to have the safe-sex discussion?" she asked. "I haven't been around much lately, if you know what I mean." It was close to the truth.

"Well, I'm—I've slowed down a bit, too," he said, not close to the truth at all, but why alarm her. "But I'm okay, really. You'll have to take my word for it. And I'll use a condom. Two or three or ten if you want. Is that enough?"

"I guess it will have to be, because I want you more than I've ever wanted anything," she said.

"Yes," he whispered, barely able to speak, his body a primitive thing, his mind gone. Naked, she was graceful and abandoned, taking him in her hand and mouth and deep into her body. He shook with desire, fearful that he could not hold back, would fail her. He ate her for a long time, until she cried out again and again, her orgasm rippling against his mouth, and unable to hold back another second, he positioned her under him, pushing her legs wide apart, and slid into her as far as he could go. For a second they held still, in suspended animation. He grasped her wrists and held her arms high over her head, looking down at her, the muscles of his arms trembling as he pulled back, held, and pushed forward slowly, slowly. Her eyes were nearly closed, her mouth open, the expression a wild passion, like rage, like fear; she grasped his buttocks in her hands and pulled him farther into her, until he could hold back no more and exploded in terrifying ecstasy.

Art slept, awakening from time to time, astonished and grateful to find Margo by his side. The rush of emotions was disconcerting. He had no desire to get up and flee. No, this was different, oddly important.

Margo, in a light sleep, tossed and dreamed, sometimes about the people at the hospital, then an old recurring dream about her ex-husband Michael, in which he returned to her. In the dream she experienced a transcendent joy, a pleasure that moved slowly out through her arms and down into her belly and legs, until she actually felt the slow-motion ripples of a half-conscious orgasm. The sensation woke her but faded quickly. She was relieved to see Art sleeping at her side. She smiled and cuddled against him.

9

Art stepped warily through the door of the small boutique. Delicate wisps of women's lingerie hung from tiny hangers over his head. He brushed at them like cobwebs, embarrassed by the sensation, as if he were intruding on the private intimacies of strangers. A saleswoman asked him if he wanted any help and he shook his head. What if she thought he was buying it for himself? Why had he come in here at all? He was reminded of the humiliating trips to the drugstore for his aunt Ida, when he was forced to *ask for*—not merely purchase—Kotex. The large, not the small. The giant, economy, steamer-trunk-size box, so big they barely had a bag for it.

Shaking off the memory, thinking instead of Margo's warm pale thighs enclosing him, he leafed through the large flat cardboards to which samples of silky merchandise were displayed like pinned butterflies. He wanted to buy her something perfect and elegant, but he realized that although he was drawn to the more tawdry red-lace styles, she might prefer one of the smooth peachy things. He was unsure whether this was the right sort of item to be buying at all after only five weeks of seeing each other. Yet, for him, five weeks was a long time, a veritable lifetime.

"For your lady friend?" the saleswoman asked.

"Yes," he said, feeling his face grow hot.

"What is her coloring?"

"Uh. Blond. Very light."

"How about this?" She proffered a shell-pink teddy of delicate satin.

"That's fine. I'll take it."

"I might need to know the size."

"Oh. Um, smallish, slim."

"A small."

"Yes. I guess."

"Will this be cash or charge?"

"Cash. Listen, do you think this is a good color? She's very light blond."

"I think she'll love it."

As she wrapped it, first in tissue paper, then in a small pearly-white box, and finally in a tiny shopping bag with the store's logo, Art glanced around. The only other customer was a woman, and he found himself wondering if she was buying for herself. She was attractive, dark-haired and tanned, and he could easily envision the black bikini panties she was regarding pressing against her dark thatch of pubic hair. She looked up and caught his eye, and he stared past her, as if he had just seen something fascinating on Columbus Avenue.

Outside with his purchase, he felt a little silly with the dainty bag, the way he felt when women asked him to hold their purses while they rearranged scarfs or coats or put on lipstick. He held it gingerly between thumb and forefinger, then abruptly folded the bag over and stuffed it into his jacket pocket.

He walked down Columbus Avenue lost in a medley of sexual fantasies. Each night with Margo—and there had been more and more of them over the past month and a half—was indelibly stamped in his sensual memory. And yet she was not a wildly passionate woman; she was not demonstratively verbal or daring. Her sensuality was low-key, as if she directed their lovemaking from a corner of her brain and remained ever vigilant. He had asked her, more than once, what she thought about when they fucked. She smiled and said. "You don't want to know."

Of course, that made him want to know even more, but he knew that if he pursued it, she would close up or simply shut him out, as she had done on several occasions. Once, when he was late to meet her, she had not been waiting for him when he finally reached her apartment. There had been no good reason for his lateness, it was his own disorganization that had delayed him, but he *had* arrived after all, which, as far as he was concerned, was the important point. But she had gone, and he spent that afternoon alone, wandering the city until it was time to go to Jack's and play, feeling unjustly punished.

He had decided he would never call her again, but by midnight his loneliness, helped along by a string of melancholy ballads and several whiskeys, had gotten the better of him, and he'd dialed her number from the club's pay phone in the back next to the cigarette machine. Getting her answering machine only incited him to keep trying, over and over, hanging up each time he heard her recorded message. Was she there, listening? Or was she out with someone else, lying on another man's bed with that inscrutable near smile and her eyes half-closed to catlike slits.

Last time they had made love—two nights before—he had undressed her with slow control, keeping her standing in the center of the room, the lights ablaze, while he told her everything he was going to do to her, and some things he knew she would never allow. "Oh, really," she'd said, licking her lips slightly, until he bent down and tasted her himself, kneeling before her but keeping the illusion of being in control by clasping her wrists behind her back. Come on, come on, he'd urged as she got closer, a sheen of sweat on her naked body; he wanted her to explode, to go crazy, but she internalized it, shuddering and shaking but not allowing him the satisfaction of her unfettered cries. And he had been the one to groan helplessly, as soon as she touched him, which she did with such cool precision that he was instantly immobilized.

He was delighted at the way her eyelashes cast tiny shadows on the delicate skin beneath her eyes. The curve of her abdomen and the feel of her inner thighs stirred him profoundly; he would be almost unable to move, let alone enter her, until she pulled him over her like a wayward blanket and absorbed him. Grasping in the dark, he was possessed by new and strange terrors that fled only when he was at the height of sensation.

He would leave her exhausted in body and spirit, go home to his tiny, drab sublet to sleep the day away and sometimes, if he didn't have to work, into the night and the next day, because if he was not to see Margo, he could not think of a reason to be out in the world.

He felt as if he had been hypnotized, taken over by unknown forces that could be turned on and off outside of his own will. Being in her presence elated him more than any drug he had ever taken, and the feeling hung over for hours afterward, compelling him to sit at the piano until his neck ached and his hands stiffened, his brain burning with new songs, fragments that came at him so rapidly, like a meteor shower, he could barely keep up with them. But when the agitation waned, it went so quickly that he was plunged into a black despair.

* * *

With the gift from the lingerie shop in his pocket, he walked toward Lincoln Center and sat on the edge of the fountain. The day was unseasonably warm for late October, and they had decided to go to the Bronx Zoo, because she had never been there. He would have much preferred to spend the day in her bed.

He had time to kill, for a change. Time always confounded him, shutting its spiteful door in his face just as he was arriving, or stretching itself languidly when he longed for it to pass quickly. In ten days he would have to leave his sublet, and he had not yet found a new place. He hated looking for an apartment, studying the newspaper ads, with their misleading and incomprehensible abbreviations; the demeaning interviews at real-estate agencies. They looked at him with frank contempt when he told them how little he was able to pay a month. And then the interviews with subletters, touring their tacky little studios and cramped 1 BRs, with them staring him up and down and asking rude questions, as if he were taking a lie-detector test. Of course, most of his answers *were* lies, but what was his alternative in this crazy city?

Margo's apartment was comfortable. On two occasions she had left him there while she went off to work. He padded around exploring her refrigerator, more stocked than his own, although not exactly bountiful; peering into her two closets. The one in the living room was

stuffed with coats, the shelf above a teetering
pile of hats, scarfs, cardboard boxes, old newspapers; the larger closet in the bedroom con-
tained most of her clothes, suitcases, more
boxes, hats, gloves, winter stuff. He had found
a box full of eight-by-ten glossy photos, of
Margo ten or twelve years before, in her actress
phase, fine blond hair ingenue-long, her expression unfamiliarly cheerful and rather vapid, like
a housewife who just used the wrong detergent
in a television commercial.

There were letters, too, most of them from
Michael, who, she had told him, was her former
husband. Grandiose, obnoxious letters, in which
he went on and on about his problems in L.A.
Art could not imagine Margo married to such a
man. Some of the letters were erotically ex-
plicit, and Art felt a profound jealousy when he
read them, but he read them nevertheless,
aroused and queasy all at once.

He had put everything back just as he found
it, closing up the cardboard boxes, stacking
them with the hats on top. Margo certainly kept
a lot of stuff. It occurred to him that she would
have to get rid of some things to make room for
his own.

Something was poking him and he awoke with
a start. The woman next to him at the Lincoln
Center fountain, an obvious tourist and mug-
ging target, complete with camera dangling
around her neck, Rockport Walkers, and a map

of the city sticking out of her half-open purse, was not pleased to have him resting his head on her shoulder.

"Oh, sorry. Do you have the time?"

She told him. He was late to meet Margo. He jumped up and sprinted to the street for a taxi.

The Bellevue lobby was teeming with people, but Margo wasn't there. He tried her office from a pay phone but no one picked up. He'd fucked up again! Why the hell couldn't she wait? Give him the benefit of the doubt. He wasn't sure what to do, so he paced the lobby irritably. A Hispanic family, a mother and three grown women who appeared to be her daughters, huddled together in some kind of collective grief. The mother sobbed inconsolably while the other women gathered around her in a huddle.

Just as he was about to give up in despair, the elevator door opened with a ping. Margo was inside, behind an orderly pushing a gurney bearing a white-sheeted ancient woman, her ashen cheeks sunken. Art had to wait while the orderly maneuvered the gurney out of the elevator, a painfully slow process. He was forced to look at the woman on the gurney, and decided that life was no longer worth living in that condition. It would never happen to him. He would die young and spectacularly. He used to think that dying young was something you did in your twenties. Now it looked as if forty would be just fine.

"I came down before but you weren't here," Margo said, not kissing him hello.

"I know. I'm sorry. I'm sorry."

"Actually, I had a lot of work to catch up on." She didn't look at him and he knew she was annoyed at his lateness, despite her words.

Art rarely took the subway, considering its squalor a reminder of all the disappointments possible in life, but Margo insisted that it was the quickest way to get to the zoo, and since they were already late. . . .

They studied the map that pinpointed the zoo. He pulled her close to him and kissed her neck, under the fine blond hair. At first she kept her aloofness, but he made her laugh and she relented, forgiving him for his lateness, all his transgressions, real and imagined. They sat close together like teenagers, her leg draped casually over his knee. He was impossibly happy.

"Excuse me, ladies and gentlemen, but please give me a few minutes of your time."

Art looked up from nuzzling Margo and saw a panhandler at the end of the car, shuffling toward them. He was white and perhaps forty years old, wearing old dungarees that looked suspiciously distressed to Art. A bandage was wrapped loosely around his upper arm with three small red splotches, and a similar one tied bandanna-style around his forehead. His tattered sneakers were unlaced and ragged and he held out a cardboard cup.

"I'm a Vietnam veteran who was injured in the service of my country—"

"Looks like he just got back," Art remarked. Margo glared at him.

"I want to work but I have been unable to find a job and I'm forced to depend on your help to pay my medical bills. Any donation would be appreciated. Thank you very much." He walked down the aisle holding out his cup. Margo quickly took two quarters out of her bag and dropped them in. The man got off at the next stop.

The train began to move again.

"Good afternoon, ladies and gentlemen, I was burned out of my home and have no place to live." This one was young and black, wearing a ski cap that stuck up over his head, jeans, brand-new Avia sneaks, and a torn denim jacket. "I have a wife and three little children living in a shelter and we are trying to save up for a home. Please help me. Please!"

As he passed by, Art said, "Sorry, we saw the first show."

Margo gave the man three dimes, all she had left in change.

"For heaven's sake, Art, do you have to be so mean?"

"All those guys are a scam. They train them in some panhandler-training school."

"How do *you* know?"

The train came out of the tunnel onto elevated tracks and rattled over the South Bronx, the empty weedy spaces where buildings had once been, acres of broken glass and tumbling concrete, windows like hollow-eyed ghosts. He worried that bands of ghetto rapists would board the train and attack Margo, forcing him to watch helplessly.

He felt for the gift in his pocket but decided that this was not the time and place to give it to her.

They reached their stop. As they were getting off, they heard, from the subway car, "Good afternoon, ladies and gentlemen. I just got out of the hospital after a serious cancer operation. My family is dead, my—"

The doors slammed shut.

The zoo was crowded for a weekday. They had forgotten that it was Columbus Day. He looked with dismay at the numerous families with their strollers and squealing children.

"Let's get a beer," he suggested.

"Now? We just got here." She headed off down the path, and he followed dutifully.

"Ah, beautiful!" she exclaimed at the sight of a flock of brilliant coral flamingos, huddled on a small island under drooping willows. Margo "oohed" at the sight of frolicking polar bears in their icy pond.

Another couple sauntered by, the woman in tight toreador pants and high thin heels. The man led her by the hand, tugging her along as she stumbled.

WILD AGAIN 109

"Imagine wearing shoes like that," Margo remarked, smug in her Nikes. "The higher the heels, the lower the class."

"And this from a woman who gives to panhandlers?"

"I just give them the benefit of the doubt."

They clustered with the crowd at the fence to view the gorillas. The animals sat steadfastly on the grass, picking at one another, staring out placidly and without rancor, fat gray bellies hanging over their folded legs and far more dignified than the pushing, chattering humans who stared with wonder or disdain.

They bought overpriced terrible pizza from the snack stand and sat on the grass eating it. Margo told him that she was trying to be a vegetarian. "Red meat doesn't tempt me," she stated, lowering her voice, as though nearby animals might overhear.

"How about the reptiles?" she said, finishing the last of her pizza and folding napkin and paper plate into her empty plastic cup. She glanced around for a trash can.

"How about we go back to the city and play hide-the-snake at your place?"

"Oh, crude, very crude." She kissed him as if she were chastising him, but he stayed with it and the kiss deepened. "Come on," she said, finally drawing away. "Reptiles."

"Crustaceans," he said, and they both laughed.

She rose and took their debris over to an overflowing garbage can. He followed, brushing grass off his jeans.

"Margo," he began, then stopped himself.

"Yes?"

"We should get a place. Together. You know."

She drew back slightly, blinking. She paused, her mouth open, as if she were about to say something and the words were stuck. She closed her mouth and scratched her cheek with one finger. "But it's only been . . . a month?"

"Five weeks."

"Where would we ever find an affordable apartment that's big enough?"

"They're out there if you look."

"I don't know," she said. "I've gotten so private, living alone, such a creature of habit, I don't know if I could ever live with another person again. It isn't that I don't care a lot for you, because I do . . . but I really know so little about you. I've never even been to your place."

"You haven't missed anything, believe me."

"For all I know you could be living with three other women."

"I am. That's why I'm always late. I have a wife and six kids in Great Neck."

"I once went out with a man I'd met at a party," she said. "I really liked him and I thought maybe this was it. He had money, too, and he took me to a really chichi restaurant. When we were leaving, I dropped my scarf, and when he leaned over to pick it up, his wedding ring fell out of his jacket pocket. That was the end of that, except that now I always arrange to drop something on a first date."

"Here," he said, turning out his pockets. Change fell onto the grass. A pigeon foraging nearby hopped over and pecked at a quarter and, with a baleful glance at Art, flew away. "No wife. No kids. And soon, no apartment."

"What do you mean?"

"Because the lease is up. It's a sublet."

"And where are you moving?"

He didn't reply.

"And you thought you might move in with me. That's just great."

This was going all wrong. "No, it was just . . . I want to be with you all the time . . . and the way things are timing out, I just thought . . . never mind, I've got another place lined up, it's not like I'm going to be on the street. . . ." Which was exactly where he was going to be if he didn't get organized.

The pizza was backing up and burning him from the inside. He lit a cigarette, noticing that his hand was unsteady. He brought it down to his side so that she wouldn't notice.

"Hey, it was just an idea, a crazy notion," he joked. "I'm just a wacky kind of guy!" He pulled out the map of the zoo grounds and studied it. "The reptile house is here." He pointed. "And the World of Darkness is over there, not very far." He stood up. "But first, a beer. 'Make it

one for my baby and one more for the road,' "
he sang.

He ordered the large beer and drank it down
fast, the foam clinging to his upper lip, ordered
another one, and downed it, too. Margo stood
by watching him, a dismayed expression on her
face.

The World of Darkness housed the nocturnal
animals. At first he couldn't adjust his eyes to
the dimness. The hall was stuffy, noisy, packed
with shrill families. People bumped into each
other as they tried to see. Gradually his vision
adapted as they came upon a glass-enclosed
replica of a forest at night. Inside, bats leaped
and swarmed, feeding on the small insects provided for them. A chill went through Art. He
had only seen bats at camp when they occasionally swooped into the area at dusk. Veteran
campers had loved to scare the newcomers with
gruesome tales of bats flying into people's hair
and eyes and giving them rabies.

"Aren't they amazing?" Margo said, trans-
fixed.

"Wonderful." He took her hand and led her
down to the next showcase.

Tiny mice scurried in and out of rocks; more
bats of different shapes and sizes; tunneling
moles with sightless eyes.

Art began to sweat. Rather than muting his
anxiety, the beer merely sloshed around inside
him without direction or purpose, while the min-

uscule, blind, gnawing, scooting, swooping creatures pecked at his imagination, made his skin itch and tingle. A person bumped him from behind and he thought how easy it would be to shove back in the dark, knock someone, anyone, to the ground, step over them, and keep moving, and no one would know.

If a person had a long, thin knife, he might slip it silently between someone's ribs, the victim's cry drowned out in the cacophony of a hundred children's voices and the sighs and squeals of animals. The animals, with their feral sense, would smell the blood, and they would scrabble their way through the protective enclosures, swarm the onlookers in a wild bloody attack, tearing into them with teeth and claws and leaving bleeding carnage on the cold stone floor.

He pressed his hot face against the glass, staring into the luminous black-pupiled eyes of a leopard cat perched on a tree in its enclosure. It stared back at him. He made his hand into a claw on the glass and the cat regarded him, blinked slowly, and leaped onto a higher branch, away from him.

He pushed his way through the crowd, looking for Margo. She was watching the owls.

"I thought you'd gone," he said.

"Gone? What do you mean?"

"I don't know. Left. Gone home. I know it was stupid, but just for a second that's what I thought. I'd hate it if you left me."

"I'm not going anywhere." She sounded ex-asperated.

"I don't mean today. I mean ever."

"Well, who knows about that."

"Look, I'm sorry, I'm doing everything wrong." —

She squinted at him, took one more look at the owls, and then led the way to the exit. The light seared his eyes as they came back out into the sun.

He wasn't sure if she still wanted him, climbing up the stairs to her apartment, watching her legs move in front of him, the sensual slide of thighs and material. She nudged the Chinese takeout menus over the threshold with her foot.

"Should I stay?" he asked.

"Of course you should stay. Don't mind me, I'm just trying to fuck this up because it's important."

"So am I."

He drew her close, before she'd even taken off her jacket. He tasted the salty sweat on her cheek, pressed her against the door, and trapped her with his body. They did it right there, standing up, grabbing and panting in harmony, giggling like children when it was over too quickly.

As he left for the club later that night, too late, in fact, to get to work on time—Jack would

not be pleased or surprised—he felt in his jacket
pocket and found the gift from the lingerie boutique and realized that he had forgotten to give
it to her.

10

"Look, I just can't hack this any-more," Clancy was saying, moving nervously from one foot to the other. "I got bills and health inspectors up the waz-zoo, and if they find you crashing here, I'm fucked."

It felt like the middle of the night, although she could see through the boarded-up window in Clancy's back room that there was light out-side. One end of the blanket was wrapped around her feet, the rest of it trailing on the dusty floor. There was no way to get comfort-able on the goddamn bruise-fest of a cot, which had wooden bars on the sides that she kept roll-ing into as she slept. She rubbed her eyes and felt the sticky remains of unwashed mascara.

"So you better pack up, you know? I'm sorry, but I gotta take care of business, I gotta deliv-ery comin', and there won't be no room back here anyhow."

"Where am I supposed to go, huh? Jus' one more night, okay?"

"Can't do it, you gotta get out." He seemed even more jittery than usual.

So fine, like she really needed his lousy cot in the back, she could find a lot better places to sleep.

"What about my money?"

"I paid you already."

"The hell you did. I gave out those fucking fliers all last night and the night before and if you think—"

"Aright aready." He dug in his jeans and came up with some bills, handed them to her. She counted carefully. It was no fortune, but at least she'd have the time to find herself a decent job and maybe buy some new shoes.

She packed her stuff in two shopping bags. Clancy said she could leave them there for a few more days. She assured him she had a place lined up, it was just a matter of waiting for the person to go out of town again.

Susan wandered into Jack's in the late afternoon and found it nearly deserted. A bartender she'd never seen before changed her dollar bills into quarters, which she stacked up by the phone. The first few calls were a waste of money. Nobody had space to put her up, even for a night. People really sucked when you got down to it. There was no answer at Gloria's, a go-go dancer who often needed someone to stay in her East Village apartment when she was away on jobs. Joey, a small-time drug pusher, wasn't at the first of two numbers Susan tried. The other was disconnected. She'd probably have to go up to the tenement in Harlem to find him. The few other so-called friends she managed to track down had a lot of fucked-up excuses why they couldn't find room for her, from unexpected guests to nosy landlords to contagious diseases.

There was a lot of noise in her head today, an annoying low rumble of sound. Sometimes it started without warning, going on and on all day and night. The noise seemed to come from behind a wide white wall, which she had first visualized in a dream. The wall was made of material that looked like Styrofoam, only harder, so that if you could scrape at it with your fingers, tiny pieces might crumble off, but it was so thick you could never get through. Behind the wall, which she saw from a distance, were people furiously trying to escape. Their arms and legs flailing in an endless, desperate struggle, and their moans and cries swelled into a roar of sound that often muffled her thinking.

She stood by the phone at the end of the bar and tried to sort it all out. She needed three things: a place to stay, a job, and new shoes. But the more she thought, the more impossible everything seemed, especially the shoes. What style would she buy? Something pretty that would hurt her feet? Or something comfortable that made her look stupid and stumpy? She slumped over the phone, weak and discouraged.

If she were someone else, she wouldn't be in such a mess and she would have a good life. Other people's lives were smooth, confident rivers into the future. Effortless, they seemed. Jobs. Boyfriends. Money. It all came to them. While there was something very wrong with her life. Something cursed and stagnant.

She left Jack's, stepping into glaring, chilly sunlight. Even the weather confounded her. Everybody said the world's outer layer was destroyed and that was why the weather was strange, but they laughed about it and went on, while she became stupefied in the heat, terrified in the cold, infuriated by the wind, buffeted from one state of being to another without her permission.

Art Glenn's picture was in the window, and for a moment she felt better, a sigh of relief releasing the knot in her body. He liked her. He talked to her, which must mean that she was all right.

Meandering a few blocks down the avenue, she spotted a sign in a boutique window: "Help Wanted Immediately."

Susan tried the door but it was locked. She could see people inside, so she knocked on the glass. A buzzer sounded and the door clicked open. Everyone in the store—a customer, a cashier, and a saleswoman—turned to look at her as if she had come to rob them.

"May I help you?" the saleswoman asked.

"I—you got a sign in the . . . uh, you got a job . . . ?"

The woman, who was maybe a year or two older than Susan, was dressed all in black, a long silk tunic over calf-length spandex leggings. Her eyes were ringed with black like a raccoon and her magenta hair was crew-cut. She raised one painted-on eyebrow.

"Have you had any sales experience?"

"Uh, yeah. Lots."

"Where?"

"Where? Uh, I sold tickets at a movie theater." She didn't add that it was a porn theater and that she'd been fired after half a day because she kept getting mixed up between Pornplexes One and Two.

The cashier, a thin boy-man wearing a T-shirt that said, 'Same Shit, Different Day,' whispered audibly, "Get the net."

The person who had appeared to be a customer started rearranging clothes on the racks and Susan realized that she worked there, too. So why the hell did they need anyone else?

"I meant, have you had any experience selling clothes?" snapped the raccoon.

"I guess not. But I could learn, I guess." If these bozos could do it, so could she.

"Why don't you leave us your name and number and we'll give it to the manager when he comes in?"

Since she didn't have a number, she just left them to their amusement. She paused and gave them all The Look before exiting. Who would want to work there, anyway?

A few blocks on, she came to a coffee shop with a "Help Wanted—Waitress" sign posted.

She could be a waitress, easy. Write down people's orders on a pad and go get the food out of the kitchen. Big fucking deal.

The place wasn't especially busy that time of day and the counterman went in the back and got the owner. He came out in a soiled white apron, a pencil behind his ear. He was thickset, with a wide, greasy mustache and an accent.

"You work place like this before?" he asked, looking her up and down.

"Sure. All the time."

"Where?"

"In . . . uh, the Village."

"My cousin Cosmos' place?"

"Sure, yeah, your cousin Cosmos."

"You lyin'. Ain't no place like that."

"I bet there is, someplace in the world. And I bet you have a hundred cousin Cosmos."

"I'm a busy man, I don't need no smart-ass bitch—"

"Fuck you—"

"—the fuck outta my restaurant—"

Turning to the customers, she called loudly.

"Check your food for roaches!" as a meaty hand on her back pushed her out the door.

Okay, so this wasn't a good day to look for a job.

Back at Jack's, she persuaded Gordon, who had just come on duty, to give her a rye and ginger ale, which she nursed until people started coming in after work. She played the jukebox with her remaining quarters, listening to Willie Nelson sing "Always on My Mind" and thinking that she preferred the way Art Glenn sang it, without the twangy sound.

The bar got so crowded, she was gradually nudged to the end and eventually to the wall near the bathrooms, where she stood immobile, empty glass in hand, pretending she belonged, listening to the hours pass in the conversations around her, the music on the jukebox, and, at long last, Art Glenn himself at the piano.

That was when she got her inspiration: she would stay with Art. An important entertainer like himself would be sure to have a big, wonderful apartment, with a grand piano and a fireplace. Susan envisioned herself curled up on a fur rug, listening to Art play special songs only for her. They would be in a penthouse, and the lights of the city would sparkle far below. He would give her champagne in an expensive glass and sing a song called "Susan Starlight."

She would sing, too, and he would say, "Oh, Susan, besides great beauty, you have the most enchanting voice. I will make you a star."

And she would say, "And when I am famous, you will play for me in my concerts at Carnegie Hall and the Hard Rock Café—"

"Miss. *Miss.*"

Jack the owner was looming over her.

"I think it's time you either got a refill or moved on."

"I just got here."

"You heard me, miss, now we've been very patient."

"I'm a special guest of Art Glenn's."

"Uh-huh."

To prove her point she edged away from Jack and over to the piano. She waited for him to look up, and when he did, she smiled and said hello.

"Hi," he replied.

"So, how's it goin'?"

"Just fine."

His hair fell across his forehead and she wanted to reach over and push it back. It was the kind of thing she would be able to do when they were alone in his penthouse.

"Uh, listen, I was wondering. . . ."

He shook his head slightly and kept playing. When he had finished, he got up from the piano, taking his glass with him.

"Uh, Art?"

"Yeah, honey, how's it going?"

"Fine, I—uh—"

"Great. I'll be back in twenty." He pushed

through the crowd and she saw him go to the phone.

She would have to talk to him later. And she would have to wait outside, since Jack was still giving her a nasty eye from across the room.

At least it wasn't too chilly outside. She sat on a parked car a few doors down from Jack's, until the car's owner came along and told her to get off, like her butt had scratchy thorns on it or something. She went and sat on another car.

She wished she had a drink or a hit of coke or even a beer, but she would have that later, at Art's place.

At one in the morning he came out and put his hand up for a cab. Susan started to walk toward him but he had shut the door before she reached him. His cab drove off. On impulse, she put her hand up, too. One of the many cabs rattling past screeched to a halt.

"Follow that taxi!" she said.

"Wha?"

"Go! Go!" she yelled at the driver, whose name on the ID card read "Ahmahl Jehed" in some strange lettering. Art's taxi had stopped at the light, giving Susan time to explain to Ahmahl very slowly that she wanted to go where that taxi was going. He shook his head and said something about American movies, but set off when the light turned green. Susan opened the window, enjoying the sensation of the breeze on her face and the view of the night city from a taxi.

They traveled downtown for a long time, finally turning left on Twentieth Street. Art's cab pulled up at the curb and he got out.

Susan hollered, "Stop! Stop here!" and Ahmahl slammed on the brakes several doors past Art's cab. Susan twisted around to see Art going into one of the buildings. She jumped out.

The driver called out, "Hey, you pay fare!" He got out of the cab and began to chase her down the street. She sprinted around the corner, the opposite direction from where Art had gone, so that he wouldn't see the commotion and recognize her. That would be all she'd need, for him to think she was trouble.

She darted into a doorway on Eighth Avenue. Ahmahl came around the corner, looking this way and that, but he didn't see her in the shadows. He wiped his forehead and muttered something to himself. He went back around the corner and a minute later she saw his taxi drive away.

Her heart was pumping hard in her chest and she felt a lift of adrenaline like she used to get when she did drug drops for Joey. Quickly she dashed around the corner, into the building Art had entered.

There were only eight mailboxes and they all had names on them but none said "Glenn." She read them again, carefully, just to be certain.

Susan went back outside, unsure what to do

next. She crossed the street and stood under a scaffolded building opposite so that she could look up at the windows. She wanted to scream with frustration: he was *in* there, but she didn't know where.

There was movement in the window on the fourth floor, the top floor. She squinted to see better. A woman was standing there. Susan could make out a halo of light blond hair around her face. A man came up behind her and they embraced. The man was Art Glenn.

Oh, so that was it. She stepped back, leaned against the building, feeling breathless and worthless. The noise in her head rose again like a wave. She heard herself breathing, from the inside, a shallow panting. The people trapped behind the Styrofoam wall in her head were crying out and she didn't know how to silence them.

11

Exhausted from a long night at the shelter, where she and another volunteer stayed awake to keep tabs on the "ladies," and that coming on top of two days with Art, Margo sat limply on the couch, too weary to feed herself or to get into bed.

The stale smell of cigarette smoke was in her hair. Although the church basement was swept out and mopped daily, by the end of a night, the toilets reeked, smoke hung in the air, and the poverty and despair left an invisible but oppressive vapor that clung to her skin. She needed to take a long, hot bath. And that only made her think about the women who had left the shelter at seven in the morning to face another day of killing time on the streets and in the train stations and bus terminals.

The first time she stayed at the shelter as a night monitor, she had come home astonished by her own good fortune. She explored her apartment, the very same place she had found confining and hopelessly drab only the day before, as if she were seeing it for the first time, as if each of her meager possessions were treasures. Her own television set was miraculous, as were her stocked refrigerator and clean white sink and warm, silky bed. She wept, uncertain why she deserved any of it.

Why her?

Why the fuck not? Art would argue.

She had welcomed her monthly night at the shelter this time. It helped purge her mind and body of the purely sexual creature she was transformed into at his touch, or even a soft murmur, a particular look.

When she was with him, her own life was submerged, and it could take her hours, days, to reclaim it. After Art, she'd find she was exasperated by the drudging demands of real life, in a state of agitated boredom like a junkie coming down. He left souvenirs of himself all over: Marlboros in the ashtrays, the toilet seat up, cups of coffee half-drunk and turned black and cold. He was constantly bringing things to read—as if they had the kind of relationship that encompassed a cozy evening at home, each buried in a book. She never saw him read any of the sports magazines and daily tabloids he scattered on her floor.

Margo glanced around the room, willing herself the strength to get started, at least tidy up before she collapsed into sleep for the day. Once she got into the shower—she hadn't the energy to scour out the tub and run a bath—she felt reenergized. In her terry robe, wet hair wrapped in a towel, she went about the apartment restoring order.

She really didn't mind the picking up, it gave her some place to focus her rattled energy. As she went about the apartment, she felt him all around her and in her body, her skin holding the lingering sensations of sex. She touched the reddish patch by her mouth, where hours of kissing had roughed her skin, and placed her hand down over her belly, and lower, where she was both sore and satiated and where, at the mere thought of him, she started moistening again.

Just as her body had been taken over, so was her mind a mélange of his stories, a mix of fact and fiction she could not begin to sort out. The stories of his life. Sad stories. Ridiculous stories.

She leafed idly through a teetering pile of mail she'd neglected over the past few days and ran back the messages on her answering machine.

My life, she thought, trying to remember what it had been like before Art.

She returned the three-day-old call from her friend Sarah, a divorced nurse with whom she often commiserated.

"So how's the greatest relationship of the late-twentieth century?" Sarah wanted to know.

"Relationfuck, you mean."

"Whatever."

"Extraordinary. Hopeless. Exhausting. Take your pick."

"Sounds fine to me."

"Oh, it is, it is." She ended the call quickly, explaining that she had a lot of work to catch up on. She'd see Sarah in the clinic and they'd figure out when they could grab a few minutes to really talk.

Then she dialed the Homeless Coalition Office and asked for Gregory Sanders, the group's organizational and spiritual leader. The sound of Gregory's rational voice was an oasis of sanity after two days with Art.

"Hi, I got your message."

"Margo, great! We'll see you tonight?"

"Wouldn't miss it for anything. When do I ever get a chance to get dressed up?"

Their organization was being given an award and a hefty check from some charity group.

"You'd look gorgeous in anything," he said.

"Thanks, Gregory. See you later."

Still restless, she put a record on the stereo. Everyone else had CDs, but she loved her old albums. James Taylor. Early Elton John. Bonnie Raitt.

"Sometimes," Art had said, "music hurts too much."

She knew what he meant. "So how do you play it night after night?"

"I disassociate."

"You seem so absorbed in it."

"Sleight of hand. Sleight of mind."

"Really."

"Sometimes I get flashbacks, you know the way people get LSD flashbacks?" he said. "Or maybe it's déjà vu. But it's like time collapses and I'm someplace else. Maybe I'm back in the first bar I played at, when I was sixteen or seventeen. That was right after I left home. Well, not exactly home, but where I lived longer than anywhere else."

"Where was that?"

"With my grandparents. In Brooklyn. After my mother died."

"You never told me your mother died."

"What did you think happened to her?"

"I—I don't know. You never really said."

It was late at night and there was very little sound from the outside, the kind of soft silence that sometimes comes over the city when it snows. Margo went to the window. Sure enough, there were large wet flakes coming down. A freak, early-November snow.

"Look," she had said to Art, who was still lying in bed, a sheet over his lower body, "snow."

"Hey, that's weird, because it snowed *that* night, too."

"What night?"

"The night she died. My mother."

"Oh." She wanted to ask him more questions but held back because in the past, whenever she'd asked about his life, he'd put her off with a joke and change the subject.

"At least I think it did. There was always snow in Cleveland that winter, so maybe it was already there, I forget. My mother, my fucking mother. Lila Noone. The Lovely Lila Noone, Queen of the Road. I was twelve and she was fucking around with this guy, this club owner? And one night I found them together and we had a fight and she never came back."

"Noone? Is that your real name?" She was always startled by how little she really knew about him, when she knew every detail of his body.

"No. That was *her* name."

He got out of bed, wrapped himself in the flannel robe Margo had bought for him to wear at her place, and lit up a cigarette. Margo automatically waved at the air, coughing a little.

"I'm sorry, I'll smoke by the window."

"No, it's okay, really. Go on."

But he went into the living room anyway; the bedroom window didn't open easily. She followed him, reluctant to be physically removed from him for long. She wanted to feel the reassuring warmth of his skin against hers, but he continued to pace restlessly, talking in a quiet, almost detached tone.

"When I was twelve, she was singing at this place in Cleveland and one night I found her with her boyfriend in his office. She was on her knees, you know? So I ran out real fast and she comes after me and tries to apologize but I blew up at her. I said some really mean stuff, I wanted to hurt her bad, told her she had no talent, shit like that. I ran down the road, I didn't know where I was going, I was just running, until some guy who worked for her boyfriend came by in his car to pick me up and take me home, before I froze to death out there on the road.

"I remember I got stoned—for the first time— with this guy, Vinnie. He was this goombah schmuck. We were out in the motel parking lot in his car 'turning on,' that's what he called it, he said, 'You wanna turn on?' and since I didn't know what the hell he was talking about and I didn't want to look like an asshole, I said 'sure' and next thing I know we're smoking grass. I knew what that was, although I hadn't tried it yet, I mean I was only twelve. So by the time I got into my room, I was pretty zonked. And starving. But there wasn't much to eat, I guess, and this wasn't exactly a fancy place with room service. It was just some lousy motel out on the highway."

Art paused at the ashtray on the windowsill, crushed out his cigarette, and lit another. The snow was striking at the window now, in big melting flakes.

"I was really pissed off at her. My mother, that is. You know that kid feeling when you wish they were dead or maybe they'll come back and find *you* dead and that'll serve them right?

And then, I don't know, I careened off the walls for a while—in my head anyway—and I guess I went to sleep.

"I had this weird dream about a machine—like a snowplow—that went down the highway real slow, pushing everything out of its way. Cars, people, telephone poles. Everything just fell in its wake. And it kept pushing this huge pile of debris that got bigger and bigger, and there were people caught up in it and they were yelling and you couldn't even see if there was a driver in the plow-thing, it was just this monster.

"And then I woke up. Someone was banging the hell out of the door. It was Vinnie, and behind him were a couple of cops, looking real grim.

"It was confusing. I was still half in the dream, groggy from the grass, and I see these cops and all I can think of is that they've come to arrest me for the grass. Somehow Vinnie'd gotten caught and turned me in."

He coughed, looked at the cigarette, and said with a short laugh, "I gotta quit one of these days." He sat down on the windowsill, his voice low and hoarse, so that she had to strain to hear him.

"But then one of the cops says, 'I'm afraid we have bad news about your mother. She died in a car accident this morning. We need you to come down to the station for a little while.' And I swear to God, for a minute there I'm actually relieved because I'm not going to be arrested. I mean, it doesn't sink in what they're telling me.

"So I get into the patrol car and it all seems kind of exciting, like an adventure, they turn on the car siren and we're going *eeh-aah eeh-aah* down Euclid Avenue and I'm looking out for the snowplow monster. I keep thinking it has something to do with all this about my mother. So we get to the police station and there's a friend of my mother's, this cocktail waitress, and apparently she's identified the body so I don't have to. And I'm just sitting there, drinking a Coke and waiting to wake up. The cocktail waitress—I think her name was Chris—she says how my mother's boyfriend must've lost control of the car, he was driving too fast, and veered off the road and smashed into the wall of a construction site."

He stopped and for several minutes there was no sound in the room except for the quiet hum of the refrigerator, the patter of snow on the window. Margo took a shallow breath and even that hurt.

Art stood up from the windowsill.

"That's one version. The official one that they told me. But I always thought that my mother did it on purpose, that she caused the accident. I figured they were having a fight over me or she was trying to get him to marry her or guarantee her an open-ended job at the club. Something. And he said no dice and she grabbed the wheel and ran them off the road. I like that one better, because at least she took things into her own hands."

"Oh, Art." Margo turned away, as she did when a client at work moved her unexpectedly, and watched the snow coating the edges of the window outside. "And the boyfriend died, too?" she asked.

"Oh, yeah, that was a kind of justice. Did I tell you he had these big nasty dogs? I don't know what the hell happened to them, but I kept thinking they were out there someplace, running around loose, and they would get me. I don't know. They were probably perfectly nice animals that acted mean because of their owner, but I had nightmares about those dogs for years. I don't even like to be around dogs now."

She couldn't help but smile a little, remembering Flops, the beloved, totally harmless cocker spaniel she'd grown up with.

"So I stayed a couple of days with Chris, until my grandparents sent money for a bus ticket and I came to New York.

"The only thing is, I always wondered what that last moment was like, what it was like for her. They said it was quick, that they both died instantly, but who knows what the truth was? What else would they tell a kid? It's like I still don't completely believe in death. Maybe if I'd seen the body . . . or maybe none of us believes in it till it happens. . . . That's why I like to think she took charge. She looked into the future and it was all gray and she said, 'What the fuck. Next exit.' "

He was still for a long time. "You know, I've never talked about this to anyone. I haven't even thought about it for years."

"I'm glad you told me."

"Real life of the party, this Art Glenn, right?"

"I love you."

"What?"

"Love you. I love you."

"Sometimes lately," he went on, as if he hadn't heard her, "I can see us together when we're very old. There's never been anyone I ever thought of that way before, anyone I wanted to be with for more than a night and, if I was high enough, maybe another day and night. But I can see us."

"Us."

"Old and comfortable."

"Cranky and creaking."

"Snarling and drooling."

"If you don't quit smoking, you won't make it to old."

"Nag, nag, nag." He reached over to her. "So you love me, huh."

"Looks that way."

"Same here. I mean, I love you, not me. Never me."

"Oh, give yourself a break."

He laughed and shook his head quickly from side to side, as if he were trying to clear it.

"Margo Magill, my part-Irish rose, my lapsed-Catholic colleen."

"Recovering Catholic, please."

"Jesus, I wish you had a piano. I could definitely write a song right now. Or at least play one."

He had pretended to play the piano then, moving his fingers over an imaginary keyboard on her skin, arousing both of them until they were making love again. Now, as she finished restoring the apartment to order, she knew she already missed him too much for her own good.

She rinsed the ashtray under a hot stream of water and set it in the drainer, turned off the lights, and crawled into her bed. There was still ice clinging to the outside of the window, diamond stalactites that shimmered in the late-morning sunlight. She watched a transparent droplet hover at its tip and was asleep before it fell, sleeping until evening chilled the darkening room.

12

The main ballroom of the Trump New York Palace Hotel had been transformed into a gingham wonderland, decorated to illustrate the theme of the Sweethearts' Ball: There's No Place Like Home, a benefit for the city's homeless. Each table was covered with a checked tablecloth and matching napkins, in blue and white, or red and white. The latter, Art observed, as he wandered around looking for the piano, reminded him more of lower-priced Italian restaurants, but then, what did he know about decor or, for that matter, society affairs?

Heaped in the center of each table was a cascading bouquet of simple flowers: daisies, baby's breath, mums. And at every place setting of early-American-style crockery there rested a gold-wrapped bar of chocolate in the shape of an old-fashioned latchkey.

He found the bandstand at the far end of the

room, surrounded by a white picket fence. The gleaming white grand piano wore a large shawl, embroidered with white-on-white flowers.

"May I help you?" He turned to see an elegantly preserved woman, frozen in time at perhaps forty-five, while the clock had marched on past sixty. An emerald and diamond necklace glittered at her neck, setting off the deep green satin of her gown's plunging décolletage. Her hair was a deep metallic gold, lightly teased and lacquered into a stiff page boy. When she turned slightly to the left, he noticed that it had been artfully arranged to cover one cheek more than another.

"Are you looking for someone?" Her tone implied that deliveries were made at the back entrance. He tried his most entrancing smile and offered his hand, while trying to get a look at her camouflaged cheek without appearing to stare. "I'm Art Glenn, the piano player?" He regretted the way his statement ended in a question, suggesting there was a chance he might not be Art Glenn, the piano player.

The woman's face brightened. "Charlotte van Dessing," she said, taking his damp hand in her cool dry one. "I'm *so* glad to meet you. We've heard *so* much about you, Biffie Mayer *adores* your playing—she was at the Redmans' party— and she said we just *had* to have you tonight. Do you know many old songs, turn-of-the-century? 'Bird in a Gilded Cage' kind of thing?"

"Yes, your assistant told me what the theme

was, so I brought a couple of collections." He opened his briefcase and removed two song-books of parlor songs, gay nineties, Stephen Foster.

"Oh, that's just *perfect*, just what we had in mind. You're a genius!"

She steered him out of the ballroom and into a large foyer from which he had come. It, too, was painstakingly decorated with homey touches. A buffet table was being readied by the catering crew, hors d'oeuvres trays covered with plastic wrap. The adjoining bar sparkled with waiting champagne glasses. Charlotte van Dessing led Art to the shiny black baby grand piano in the corner, its legs sunk several inches in deep mauve carpet.

"Don't you just *love* the way everything looks?" she said, close to his ear. "Willie White is our decorator, he did the Crystal Ball last year?"

Art nodded admiringly, as though he'd actually heard of the Crystal Ball, and maybe had even been there.

"In the most divine crystal and white, like a fresh snowfall? It was breathtaking, and we raised so much money for Nancy's Just Say No campaign. She was there, of course, although Ronnie couldn't come."

She bent closer to the piano top, squinting at it. "Dusty!" she said. When she straightened up, her hair fell back slightly and Art saw that her left cheek was disfigured with old burn scars.

New skin must have been grafted on at one time.

"It's been so hectic, I have just worked my little tail off," she went on. "What with everyone wanting to sit at this table or that. You know, of course, that Betsy Bishop is feuding with Jerry Carlisle and my assistant had put them at the same table! Can you imagine?"

"There's always something, isn't there," he said, straight-faced. "But you've done such a splendid job." Jesus. *Splendid*. This was going to be fun. Confidence swelled inside him. He lifted the lid over the piano keys and placed his music on the stand.

"Well, aren't you sweet," she replied. "When Princess Sekeny canceled her whole table today, I thought: This is it, no one will come. I tried to explain to her that it's such a good cause—those poor homeless people, you know." She lowered her voice, the way white people do when they say "black" in a public place. "But she wouldn't change her mind, though she did say she'd send a check. Would you like a drink?"

"Why, that would be simply delightful," he said.

"The guests won't start arriving for another twenty minutes or so, then you'll play for about an hour out here, and fill in between the band's sets in the dining room. Everything all right?"

"Yes. Fine. *Enchanté*."

When she walked away and began talking

heatedly to one of the caterers, he realized she wasn't going to bring him the drink herself. He crossed to the bar.

Two JDs later, he settled down to play. The piano was a good one for a change. It was actually in tune. He began quietly, with a few of the oldies from the songbooks. Guests began to arrive, milling around in their finery, balancing plates and glasses. After a half hour, Charlotte came over and suggested that the old songs were sweet and everything, but weren't they just a little *down?* The party needed something a bit more lively, so he switched to Cole Porter and began working his way up from the thirties to the forties.

Charlotte's twenty-year-old daughter, Jinx, approached the piano. Even if she hadn't introduced herself, he would have noticed the younger version of the ball's grande dame in Jinx's smooth towheaded beauty, without the unpleasant scar, of course, and still a bit baby-fat plump, her generous figure set off by a wide-skirted red "Jezebel" gown. He caught an intriguing whiff of perfume when she leaned in to thumb through his songbooks, searching for a song she couldn't remember the title of.

"When was it written?" he asked her.

"Oh, maybe two or three years ago."

"Well, these songs are all from the late-nineteenth century."

"Oh!" She laughed. "Then I guess that's why I can't find it!" She walked away giggling.

His first break came when dinner was announced and the guests, now numbering some three hundred, meandered into the No Place Like Home dining room, where Dickie Dahlia and his Society Orchestra took charge of the musical entertainment. Art asked the bartender, an actor handsomer than anyone needed to be, if and where he was supposed to eat. The bartender shrugged and suggested he sit with Dickie Dahlia and the band.

Art located the musicians' table, which was as near to the kitchen as you could go without actually being a busboy. He sat alone with eleven empty place settings around him, fruit salads wilting, wine warming, watching the white-suited Dahlia pound the white piano and conduct his orchestra.

Dickie Dahlia had jet-black Grecian Formula hair and a deeply creased, tanned face, perfectly even features like an aged Ken doll. He displayed a wide capped smile as he led the band through watery renditions of big-band tunes and occasionally warbled a ballad with wobbly vibrato.

Art studied each musician and wondered if any of them liked what he was doing, or if they had long ago given up on their original dreams of being Gene Krupa or Charlie Parker or Benny Goodman. The men—they were all men—were mostly middle-aged and older, faces expressionless as they blew their horns or waited their turn. There were a couple of young guys who sat forward in the bandstand, poised for the high point of the set: their sixteen-bar solos.

When the band broke, Art took Dickie Dahlia's place at the piano, providing background to the clanking of silverware and the festive chatter. He played for twenty minutes while the band wolfed down dinner. When they returned to the bandstand, Art had nothing to do again. He didn't feel much like sitting at the empty table, so he got a fresh drink and stood in the back of the room watching.

Between courses, the party guests cavorted on the dance floor to the band's renditions of rock hits. Dickie Dahlia crooned a stiff version of "Money for Nothing." Bodies bounced up and down, side to side, color and movement shifting like a kaleidoscope. Charlotte was in the center, dancing with an elderly silver-haired gentleman who moved like a stick figure, waving his arms out to the sides. Charlotte was enjoying herself immensely, on her face the heavy-lidded pouty expression of a disco dancer, arms flailing, pelvis pumping rather rhythmically for a WASP woman of a certain age. Art imagined her in bed. She could be the oldest richest woman he might ever sleep with.

His gaze shifted to Charlotte's daughter Jinx, potentially the youngest richest woman he might ever sleep with, dancing with a tall thin man with a short haircut that crossed punk and

Aryan youth, wearing an expression of soul-deep ennui, his tux collar loosened, tie dangling limply. Jinx kept looking around to see who was watching her and eventually caught Art's eye. When her mother's partner let out a shrill "Whoop," Jinx rolled her eyes as commentary on the older generation's lack of cool.

Dickie Dahlia hammered out the last of the obligatory rock medley and sunk back into the comfortable strains of "I Love Paris" in a cha-cha beat. Art saw Jinx approaching him from the dance floor.

"Dance?" she said. Up close, the whites of her pale blue eyes showed tiny red lines from drink or fatigue or both.

"Sorry. Piano players don't dance."

"Oh, but why? You've got rhythm, you play just wonderfully."

"Well, you see," he said carefully, feeling the drinks on his tongue muscles, "most musicians never learn to dance because they're always playing while everyone else dances."

"Ooh, that's a shame, but we could try a slow one."

On the bandstand, Dickie Dahlia was enthusiastically leading the band through "April in Paris," still featuring the cha-cha.

Art asked, "Is Jinx your real name?"

She rolled her eyes at the ceiling and said very slowly, emphasizing the first syllables: "Jessica Isabella Norcross Xavier van Dessing."

"Hmm. Very clever."

"Mummy's sense of humor. I think she married Daddy for the X in his last name."

"The X?"

"He was Thomas Graham Xavier. You know. The ambassador."

"Oh, sure." He thought of asking her where her mother got the scar but decided it might be rude. And how come, with all that money, she couldn't have it fixed.

"But he kicked off and she married van Dessing. For the 'van.' His is real. Not like Claus von Bulow's."

"It's all so fascinating."

"Yes. Oh, you see that man she's dancing with? That's Bittles Stewart, the chairman of Stewart Chemical. I suppose he's next. You know, they're having a dinner party next month and I don't think they've hired anyone to play yet, and Mummy wants to keep it simple, a little cocktail music instead of a band. You'd be perfect. Would you be interested?"

"Well, yes. But of course I'd have to check my schedule."

"Of course," she said, in a slightly mocking tone.

The band finished their set. The Hispanic busboys cleared the tables and the actor-waiters began hauling out coffee and dessert on trays. Art started for the piano but Charlotte caught his eye and waved for him to stop. She didn't want him to play anymore? Had he been fired? No. Dickie Dahlia was making an announcement. It was time for the benefit part of the evening, speeches to be made, money raised for the cause of the moment.

Art returned to the table, now taken up by the band. He sat next to one of the saxophone players, a small, nervous man who kept sucking on a slivery thin reed from his horn's mouthpiece.

"Don't make 'em like they used to," the man said, turning his weaselly gaze on Art. Viewed front ways, the man's face was oddly narrow, as if it had been compressed in the birth canal. He held out the wet reed for Art's inspection.

"No. I guess not," Art replied.

The lights in the ballroom dimmed further and spotlights lit the stage. Art could barely make out the identity of the dessert that had just been placed before him. The sax player leaned over, exuding a wine-garlic breath, and asked him if he was going to eat his dessert.

"No, I don't think so. Here, go ahead."

"Thanks. No point in wasting it."

Dickie Dahlia left the stage after introducing Charlotte van Dessing, the chairwoman of the Sweethearts' Ball. She climbed the steps to the stage, clutching her voluminous skirts and shading her eyes against the spotlight. She took the microphone gingerly, tapped it as if it were a foreign thing. The applause died down.

"Good evening and welcome to our second annual Fleetwood Foundation Sweethearts' Ball." She drew back from the microphone, tapped it several more times, asking, "Is this on?" Numerous guests and most of the Society Orchestra yelled out that it was.

Art turned to the sax player. "What's the Fleetwood Foundation?" The man shrugged, his mouth full of food.

". . . introduce to you the president of the Fleetwood Foundation, Abbott Whitby!"

Whitby droned on about the Fleetwood Foundation and all its good works, the problems of the homeless, and the wonderful efforts of the Homeless Coalition, several of whose members had come tonight. Art stood up to get a drink when he saw a familiar shape.

Margo Magill. His Margo.

She was standing at the edge of the stage among the group from the Coalition.

Why hadn't it occurred to him that she might be here? Why hadn't she mentioned it? Had *he?* Yes, but all he'd said was "I've got this society gig" and she said, "I have a dinner for the Coalition." So naturally they hadn't put it together.

He started toward her, hardly able to conceal his delight as he imagined her surprise. He didn't want to walk conspicuously between the tables, so he went around the back of the ballroom and came down the far aisle that led to stage right. Margo had her back to him. He saw her turn to the man standing next to her and say something.

Art stopped.

She took the man's hand and gripped it in

front of her. He was quite tall and lean, good-looking in a clean-cut, collegiate way—the kind that would run committees and study comparative religions and live in a poor neighborhood even if he could afford better.

"... the head of the Homeless Coalition, Gregory Sanders!"

Margo's friend leaped to the stage, smiling brilliantly and waving at the applause. Art sensed a political candidate in the making, a future Congressman Sanders or Senator Sanders. Art watched Margo watch Sanders as he began his speech. She was looking at him with ... what? Admiration? Awe? Love?

She was too engrossed in staring at her idol to notice Art. He came up behind her and whispered in her ear, "What's a nice girl like you, etc. etc."

"Art! My goodness!"

"Surprise."

"Yes! Is this where you were playing tonight? That's amazing!" She turned her attention back to the stage, where Sanders was saying, "... not just better shelters but real low-income housing ..."

"Yes, isn't it," Art said. Was she sleeping with Sanders? Maybe she thought about Sanders when she was with him. Maybe that's why she refused to tell him her fantasies. Jesus, what a jerk he was.

"... my gratitude to the Fleetwood Foundation for organizing and raising so much ..."

"So, uh, can you stick around? Hear the romantic sounds of Art Glenn at the piano?"

"No, Art, sorry, we have to be at the Coalition House for a late meeting."

I'll bet you do. "With that guy?"

"What guy? Gregory? What are you talking about?"

"I thought you could at least stay around to hear me play."

"I'd love to, but—"

One of Margo's colleagues turned and glared at the two of them, placing forefinger to lips.

". . . and I'd like to thank my staff who've come along tonight and who work so hard making the Coalition a reality—Joel Baker, Les Ginsberg, Margo Magill!" The spotlight swerved and searched out the group, as Art said under his breath, "Fuck you, Margo."

"No, fuck *you*, Art."

Applause either acknowledged his outburst and her reply or drowned them out, he wasn't quite sure, but she was leaving, climbing up the steps to take a self-conscious bow. A few minutes later the Coalition's portion of the evening was up, the guests ready to get back to the serious business of the evening: partying. Gregory Sanders helped Margo off the stage. She paused in front of Art.

"I don't know what the problem is, but I can't stay and work it out now. Good night, Art."

He closed his eyes for a second, momentarily

confused from the combination of alcohol and the sour sensation of jealousy. He followed her to the hotel's grand lobby.

"Margo!" Startled lobby guests looked at them.

Sanders turned, a half smile on his face, in the middle of some witty anecdote, no doubt. The other two members of their group were already out the revolving door.

"Margo," he said more quietly, approaching. "Could we talk?"

"I don't think we've met," said the other man, putting out his hand. "Gregory Sanders."

Art hesitated, then shook hands.

"I don't have much time, Art," she said coldly. "We have to be someplace."

"Just for a second."

"I'll wait for you outside," said Sanders, walking away.

"Aren't you working?" she asked in a tight voice.

"I'm on a break. I have to go right back, but I wanted to say—" What? What did he want to say? ". . . that if this is the way you want it, then fine, fine with me—"

"Want *it*? Want *what*?"

"Us. You know. Him."

"You're drunk, Art."

"I've *had* a few *drinks*, I'm not *drunk*."

"I can't deal with this. Not now," she said. "Why are you doing this?"

"I'm not *doing* anything. I just came out to say, hey, have a swell evening."

"Oh, Art, what the hell are you doing? What do you want me to do? Just drop my whole life because I happened to run into you tonight?"

"Is he your whole life then?"

"He? Give me a break! Look, I love you but I can't deal with you. I can't even depend on you, do you expect me not to have any other friends? I never know what you're going to do—"

"Oh, so you've been thinking about this for a while, huh?"

"No! Well, yes, a little. The drinking really bothers me, you know that."

"The drinking? You've got to be kidding! That's nothing, I can stop anytime."

"It's that and . . . other things, too. I . . . look, this isn't the time or the place."

"Right, wait for me, or come back later, or I'll meet you—"

"But I have my own life to live, I can't be worrying about you all the time. Wondering if you'll show up on time or at all, if you'll be in good shape, if you've stayed out all night doing God knows what with God knows who."

"So, hey, fine, who asked you to worry about me? I can take care of myself. I've been taking care of myself for about a hundred years, and I'll go on taking care of myself for another hundred." He grinned and did a quick softshoe on the carpet. "Art Glenn: the lone wolf of the piano. For your listening pleasure!"

She smiled slightly. He wondered how this evening could have taken such a wrong turn.

"Art Glenn?" Someone was calling his name. They both turned to see Jinx sweeping through the lobby in her Jezebel-red gown. She scolded playfully, placing her hand on Art's arm. "They're looking for you. Mummy's getting nervous!"

"You'd better get back, Art," Margo said, her voice hard. "Mummy's getting nervous."

"I'll be right there. Oh, uh, Jinx, this is a friend of mine, Margo Magill, we didn't know we'd both be at the party. What a funny coincidence, huh!" How could he have even thought of fucking this little dumpling Jinx, with her smooth silly face and her creamy baby tits. Seeing her next to Margo, he was appalled at himself, simply disgusted with a libido that had a will of its own.

Margo headed for the revolving door. Art was right behind her.

"So, is this it? So long, farewell, auf Wiedersehen, good-bye?"

"We'll talk."

"That's nice, Margo, I'll be looking forward to our talk. I'm sure we can sit down and have a nice civilized discussion, a regular therapy session about why you're dumping us—"

"I'm not the one fucking this up for a change. You're doing it all on your own. Good *night*."

"And I don't give a fuck either," he called after her.

He walked back to Jinx, who was watching with undisguised amusement.

"Girlfriend?" she asked.

He felt a deep ache in his chest. "One of many, honey, one of many."

13

He couldn't see any reason to go home to a bed and a sink in a sleaze-bag building on West Fifty-first Street. Outside the Trump New York Palace at one in the morning, a fat check from the Fleetwood Foundation nestled in his pocket next to Charlotte van Dessing's card, Art looked around for a cab, but the limousines were double-parked all the way to the next block. He started walking crosstown, instinctively heading for Jack's where he was assured of a friendly welcome.

He finally caught a taxi eight blocks later and shivered the whole trip uptown and across the park. What he needed was a vacation in a warm place. He'd send Margo a postcard.

"Right," he told himself.

"You say?" asked the dark-skinned cabdriver of some Middle Eastern descent.

"Nothing. Uh, aren't you going to go up Amsterdam? It's more direct."

"Amserdan?"

"Yes, turn here. *Here!* All right, the next street that goes west."

How did these guys get hack licenses?

"Here! On the right. The right! Never mind, I'll get off by the dumpster." He handed over five bucks, resentful of giving a tip in addition to the extra fifty-cent nighttime surcharge, but too impatient to wait for change.

His sub was playing, the pianist he usually called to fill in when he had another gig. Mattie Greene was a slightly built young man with an encyclopedic knowledge of Sondheim and a shivery tenor voice. As Art entered, he heard Mattie playing "Not a Day Goes By."

What if Jack and the customers decided they like Mattie Greene better? He scanned the room, still crowded despite the late hour, and saw that no one was listening. He was relieved to see that they were just as inattentive and rude as they were when he was playing.

Gordon, a sometime playwright, was tending bar. Art had once gone to see one of Gordon's plays in a small loft space in SoHo. It was a very angry play about Vietnam, full of filthy language and death. Art had enjoyed it a lot, although the straggly minor critics who came to see it disagreed.

"Hey, Artie, what's up? You coming in even on your day off?"

"What can I tell you. I have no life."

"And look at the fancy duds! You must've been somewhere better than here."

"The high life, Gordie, I've joined the 'upper set.' "

"There was a woman in here looking for you a little while ago."

So, she'd realized she was wrong and come to find him! He knew it, knew she'd come around. Pleased, he took a sip of the drink Gordie had automatically put in front of him.

"Oh, yeah?"

"She's been in here before. A little weird. Gives out fliers or something."

The drink seemed to freeze in his throat. His voice caught as he replied, "Oh, yeah, thanks."

"I told her you weren't working tonight. If I'd known you were coming by . . ."

"No problem, Gordie. She'll be back." He dug in his pocket. "Listen, you got silver? I need cigarettes and phone change." He handed Gordie a fiver.

With a pocketful of change, he made his way to the back and got the cigarettes first. He would need them. Then he dropped in a quarter and dialed Margo's number.

Her machine answered and he nearly hung up waiting for the beep.

"Hi, Margo, it's Art. Look, I'm sorry about earlier, I was out of line. I just got so crazy, and well, I'm sorry, okay? So look, I'm up at Jack's. I just stopped in for a little while, so if you get this message, you can call me here. Or call my service. Or my place, they take messages at the desk. If you can get the clerk who speaks English. Or I'll call you tomorrow. Okay. I'm sorry, I'm an asshole, sue me, shoot me, call the asshole police. But let's not lose this, okay? Margo? Hello? Oh, I thought I heard you pick up. It was just a click in the line. You're not there listening to this are you, listening to me being a jerk on the phone? No, I'm talking to myself. I'm standing here with sawdust under my feet talking to the tiny holes of a black plastic *thing*, to a machine I can't see. It could be broadcasting my message into space or something. Martians are getting a good laugh right now. God thinks it's a real knee-slapper. I guess you're sorry you put your message tape on 'unlimited,' huh? I guess tomorrow you'll switch it back so that crazies can only talk for thirty seconds. Did you hear that Abbie Hoffman's going underground again? Joke. Okay, I'll leave you alone, I'll go home and be good for a change. I'll be incredibly boring, I'll get up early, promise. Just let me see you again. Okay?

The only problem with leaving phone messages, he thought as he hung up, was that you couldn't take them back.

". . . Isn't it rich? Are we a pair? Me here at last on the ground, you in midair . . ." He was crowded next to Mattie Greene on the piano bench, playing the right-hand part on the piano, both of them crooning away. Mattie looked at his watch and immediately segued into "It's a quarter to three, there's no one in the place except you and me. . . ."

Of course, there still were other people in the place: Gordie, Jack, counting up the night's receipts. A few late customers. A couple in the corner had been engrossed in each other for hours but didn't make the inevitable move to go home to bed, so Art figured one or both of them was married and this was it, this was all they had together. God, it was sad, it was all so fucking sad.

He sat on the piano bench next to Mattie and improvised a few notes.

"What a duo we make, Art," said Mattie, nudging Art's buttock with his own. "Now if only you were gay."

"If I were gay, I'd probably be dead by now."

"Yeah, you're right. You're too cute. You'd have gone in the first wave."

"What about you, Mattie? How come you're still here, cute guy like you?"

"It's really very simple, Arthur. I never liked to take it up the ass. Isn't that a hoot? A simple sexual preference. Don't you just love it!" Mattie's shrill laugh rose above the music.

Art saw the flier girl at the door. "Oh, shit."

"What is it?"

"This crazy chick jus' came in."

Mattie began to play "Pretty Women" from *Sweeney Todd.*

She spotted him and came over, her high heels

clicking on the wood floor. "Artie! I was in earlier. They said you wouldn't be here!" She followed him to the bar.

"I couldn't stay away, knowing there was a chance of seeing you. Still handing out those fliers?"

"I'm done for tonight, and maybe for good. This guy I met? He's lookin' for models, so he ast me to get him some pitchers."

"Dwight Gooden? Nolan Ryan?"

"Huh?"

"Nothing. Nude pictures?"

"You crazy? I wouldn't do that, it could ruin my future. Look at that Miss America, the black one, what'sername."

"Vanessa Williams?"

"Yeah. Look at what happened to her."

"She's got a hit record."

"So fucking what."

"Right. So fucking what. What the fuck is your name anyway?"

"Susan. I told you that. And you're Art Glenn: 'the piano stylings of Art Glenn,' " she said, quoting the poster outside.

"Yes. Isn't that impressive."

Susan took out her hand mirror and checked her face, inspecting it, paying particular attention to the now-faded red mark. She squeezed a tiny tube of cream and rubbed a dab into the faint smile lines that would one day outline her mouth like parentheses.

"What are you doing?" he asked.

"I don't want to get wrinkles."

"Aren't you a little young to be worrying about that?"

"Are you kidding? I'm twenty-two!" She rubbed another dab into a potential frown line between her eyebrows. "You have to prevent these things while you're young, before it's too late."

"I guess it's too late for me."

"Oh, no! You're a guy! It doesn't matter so much with guys, although it matters *some*." She put away the cream and mirror. "God, I'm so tired and thirsty."

Art waved Gordon over and asked Susan what she wanted to drink. She ordered a rye and ginger ale. Gordon brought Art another JD straight up. The clock over the bar said three, and he thought that if he could just get through this night, then everything would be all right. With enough drinks in him, even Susan would start to look good. It wasn't that she was unattractive, she was actually kind of pretty in a cheap way, wearing tight black slacks with high heels. What did Margo say? 'The higher the heels the lower the class.' Oh, well, he'd seen worse. He'd *been* with worse. Coyote ugly, Jack called them, because when you woke up in the morning with one in your arms, you'd rather chew your arm off like a coyote in a trap than be forced to wake her up and talk to her.

". . . so I moved out and I been staying with

this girlfriend, Gloria? But she went outta town for a coupla weeks, she's a go-go girl and—"

"I didn't know they still had go-go girls."

"Well, sure, whattaya think dances in those places in midtown—"

"Oh, I guess I was thinking about the ones in cages."

Susan looked at him blankly, then resumed, "I danced for a while, there's a lotta places in Jersey where you don't hafta go topless like in New York, although they try to get you to take your top off when it's late, even though it's against the law. The owners of these clubs? They take up a collection from the customers and then they lock the door, like it's a private club, you know? And the girl dances topless for a while and makes a lotta tips."

"You did that?"

"No! You crazy? This girlfriend whose apartment I'm stayin' in—well, she's really more of an acquaintance—she does it." Susan shrugged. "She got raped a coupla times," she added matter-of-factly.

"Sounds dangerous."

"Yeah. Well," she said, as if it were all in a day's work. "Excuse me," she said, getting up. "I hafta go to the little girl's."

When she was out of range, Art put his head down on the scarred wood and moaned quietly.

"Bimbo alert," commented Gordon, swiping at the bar with a cloth.

"Tell me about it. Listen, I'm heading out. Tell

her I had to run, tell her I was beamed up to another planet. Tell her anything, Gordie. And would you mind stashing my music behind the bar?" He handed over his plastic briefcase. Then, on second thought, he opened it up and removed the small package he'd been carrying around for weeks: the present he'd bought Margo and kept forgetting to give to her. This must be a symbol of the relationship, he thought dryly. The gift that was never meant to be. He stuffed it in the pocket of his tuxedo, where it made an unattractive bulge. He handed the briefcase over to Gordon.

Art waved a good-bye at Mattie, who was happily singing "Being Alive."

14

Out on the street the icy wind cut right through to his skin and he almost went back inside. He hadn't managed to achieve the balloon of good feeling he was seeking, that magic second when the booze clicked in and lifted him up out of the world.

"Artie, wait up!"

The flier girl, Susan, was running after him, wobbling on her high heels. He considered sprinting away, but his feet, squeezed into rigid black-patent-leather dress shoes, hurt too much. He paused and let her catch up.

"I don't wanna go home alone, you know?"

He remembered something from an early conversation, a husband who painted the Brooklyn Bridge in his undershirt.

"Aren't you married?"

"Nah, I lived with this guy and we got a kid but he pushed me around alla time, so I left.

The kid's with my mother in Queens. Till I can get on my feet. When my career takes off an' I'm a famous model, I'll buy a house on the island."

"What island?"

"*Long* Island, of course."

He kept walking; she trailed along, like a lost puppy. "So where do you live now?" he asked, resigned.

"I *told* you, at this friend's place, the dancer."

"Oh right."

She told him the address: a seedy street in the East Village.

Wonderful, he thought, Alphabet City. The heart of the gentrification wars.

He checked his pockets for cash and, satisfied he had enough, hailed one of a herd of cabs barreling down the nearly deserted Columbus Avenue. He helped Susan in and climbed in beside her. She gave her address to the driver, who was nearly hidden behind the clouded safety screen dividing the front seat from the back.

As soon as they were in motion, she delved into her purse and took out a tiny glass vial with attached spoon, snuffled up two nostrilsful of white powder, and handed it over to Art.

"Thanks. You've had a windfall, I see."

"Huh?"

"You won the lottery?"

"Nah, this guy, the one with the modeling agency, he gave it to me. He's a cool dude and he said this was a 'token of faith' because I was gonna be so big."

"I bet." He helped himself to some more, handed it back to her. All at once he felt enormously better. So what if the thing with Margo had fallen apart? So what if it was cold outside? He was Art Glenn and he was a brilliant musician ... his talents were appreciated by rich people who would invite him on their yachts, play their parties, deb balls, ripe young girls "coming out," whatever the hell that was. Maybe he'd even marry one of them. Like Jinx. There would be money, record contracts: *The Romantic Side of Art Glenn; Art Plays Cole; Glenn at the Carlyle;* then he'd get a cameo in a Woody Allen movie, like Bobby Short, and his songs would be published, the one he wrote for Margo a huge hit. . . .

He reached over and grabbed Susan, kissing her, probing deeply with his slightly numbed tongue.

He could still see the grand ballroom of the Trump New York Palace Hotel, all the gorgeous women and the self-assured men, the jewels and the money, nubile Jinx and lean mean Charlotte. As the dance ended, one of the young women guests fell down right in the middle of the dance floor. She wouldn't get up and her date had to try to reason her onto her feet, but she took off a pointy silver shoe and hurled it at her date instead. He went weaving out, cursing, then he threw up in the hallway, while the band played "Good Night, Ladies." The poker-faced hotel cleanup crew moved in with mops and brooms and Dustbusters, the last guests drifted off into the night, the hall emptied like someone pulled the drain plug. What a swell party it was.

He had his hands under her blouse now; she felt unfamiliar and that was good, someone new and different. He'd like to fuck this girl, fuck her brains out.

The cab stopped and the driver knocked on the partition to get their attention. Art pulled back like a child caught with his hands in his pants.

They were in front of one of three standing buildings on the street. The rest were rubbled lots where buildings had once been. Susan took out her key and started to open the front door, but it was already unlocked and opened at a slight push. The vestibule was small and foul smelling, most of the mailboxes broken and hanging on hinges. Only two of them had names pasted to the front.

He had to hand it to her. This was even worse than some of the places *he'd* lived. If he hadn't been high, he might have found it really depressing, but in his happy balloon state, he found himself wondering if there was a vacancy.

He followed her up three creaking flights, watching the sway of her behind in her tight black slacks, the thin panty line showing underneath. She stopped in front of a door with a Greenpeace sticker, fumbled around with the keys, trying one, then another before she found the right ones for the various locks. The door was a locksmith's dream, an assortment of bolts and bars.

The apartment was a small, narrow railroad flat with the tub in the kitchen, but this had been disguised with curtains of a bright flowered material. The floor in the living-room area had been partially stripped and sanded, the project stopped midway. The kitchen floor still showed layers of peeling linoleum, dating back to the tenement's origins.

In the bathroom Art discovered the apartment owner's true decorative sensibility. The walls were papered in a fuzzy red velvet, the paper curling off at the top corners, revealing old stained walls and the preserved carcasses of two cockroaches that had been trapped in the wallpaper glue. He lifted the toilet seat, one of the soft types that always mystified him— what was the point of an upholstered toilet?— and peed into the bowl, staring at a small framed piece of paper on the wall. Leaning in, he saw that it was that 1960's relic desiderata: "Go placidly amid the turmoil. . . ." and so forth. Just then, a roach was going placidly down the fuzzy red wall. Art flushed the toilet and rinsed his hands, splashed water on his face. He could taste the metallic residue of the coke dripping down the back of his throat.

Susan was sitting on the couch, smoking a cigarette and drinking what looked like whiskey from a jelly glass. The TV across the room was on, tuned to MTV. He lit a cigarette and she handed him a glass that had once been a Peter Pan Peanut Butter jar. He took a sip of cheap bourbon, grimacing.

"This is what she had around," Susan explained. "I don't usually drink at home." She had the vial of coke at hand, however, and she shared the last of the small stash of powder with Art, although he guessed she'd had a few hits while he was in the john; drug altruism only went so far. The lights were dim, mainly because there was just one lamp in the room. It rested on the side table— actually an upended carton box painted brown and refinished with some kind of imitation wood stain—the lamp base a vaguely modern clay sculpture of a nude woman. The shade was burlap brown and didn't come down far enough to mute the light bulb's glare. Leaning against the lamp was a small photo. Art picked it up and saw a pretty woman in her thirties standing on a boardwalk that might be Atlantic City.

"That's Gloria," said Susan.

Art looked around at Gloria's apartment: the cheap furniture, what there was of it, the decorating attempts, the half-sanded floor. His gaze came to rest on Susan, who was watching him carefully.

"I wish I had a piano so you could play something." He noticed she tended to overenunciate when she talked.

"That's okay, I've played enough tonight."

"I really like your playing."

He couldn't think of anything more to say, so he took her in his arms. He didn't kiss her this time; something about her mouth bothered him. Maybe it was just her grating accent. Instead, he kissed the base of her throat and reached into her blouse. She wore a frail lacy white bra that unclasped easily from the front. She removed the blouse and the bra. He bent over to kiss her breasts, then stopped.

They were well shaped, small and firm, but they had tiny dark hairs surrounding the nipples, like a circle of little curlicues.

He drew back. Did other women have hairs there? If so, did they shave? Or what?

"What'samatta?"

"Uh, nothing." He drank a slug of whiskey. It burned all the way down, mingling with the acids stirred up by his empty stomach, the residue of cocaine-tainted saliva.

On the television screen, a heavy-metal band screeched their way through a song, jumping up and down, manes of white-blond hair bouncing wildly. The camera cut dizzily from one frame to another. Art looked away, his head beginning to ache. He rubbed his eyes.

"Don'tcha feel good?"

"No, I'm okay."

"Here," she said, undoing his pants, zipping

down his fly. She took out his penis, which was as flaccid as a burst balloon. Just like his mood.

"No, that's okay." She was bending over him and he wished she'd just leave him alone. Who would ever have thought he'd turn down a blowjob? But she didn't stop, she was sucking on him hard and it hurt, her teeth scraping his skin. Jesus Christ, he thought, she gave the worst blowjob in the world. The cocaine was terrible. This apartment was terrible. What was he doing here? He was too old for this kind of dumb groping, fucked-up shit. Had to get out of here.

He pushed her away, a little rougher than he intended. She slipped off the couch.

"Hey! What'samatta with you? You got a problem?" She clambered to her feet.

"No, Susan. I haven't got a problem. I just . . . don't feel like it, all right?" He stood unsteadily, grabbing onto the lamp. It toppled over at his touch. "Oh, shit."

"You broke it, you stupid faggot, look what you did!"

She was staring at him strangely, her eyes narrowed and unblinking. He was startled by her sudden burst of anger. All he wanted to do was leave. He crossed the room to get his jacket. She was right behind him.

"You think you can fuck me over, jus' like Boyd, you can push me around and make funna me behind your back, but I'm gonna be famous an' then you'll see!"

"I'm just going to go home and get some sleep. I'll . . . I'll call you, okay?"

She grabbed at the tuxedo jacket furiously. "With your fancy clothes and your hot-shit music, you fuckin' faggot, you can't even get a hard-on!"

"For Christ sake let me—"

"Comin' in here like you fuckin' care and breakin' Gloria's lamp."

"I'll pay for it, I promise, will you just shut up!"

"—hate you all, all you hot-shit uptown slobs, you fuckers!" She was practically screaming now, a dull growling roar that swelled as she tore at the jacket, ripping the lining easily, tearing off buttons, biting it like it was everything she hated in the world.

"Jesus Christ, you stupid bitch!" He grabbed for the jacket, his only tuxedo, the one he'd saved up to buy from the rental place. He tore it away from her, fueled by his own indignant anger. He whipped the material through the air, catching her on the side of the head with the sleeve. She cringed away, raising her arms to shield her face. He whipped the jacket through the air again, crying, "Stupid stupid bitch!", seeing Margo's face saying "I can't be worrying about you all the time. . . ."

He brought the jacket down with all his strength, hitting the floor, the wall, the fallen lamp.

"Stop it!" she cried, stepping back into the

kitchen. She lost her balance as she went, and tripped over the sill, hurtled backward, falling, falling. Her head struck the edge of the table as she fell. He heard a sickening crack just before she hit the floor. And then she was still.

He stood over her, clutching the jacket, gasping for breath.

"Susan?" he whispered hoarsely.

She was frighteningly still. He moved a step closer and leaned down to touch her. He recoiled as if she were an alien thing. She was lying with her nude torso twisted forward, her face to the floor. Now he saw that a trickle of blood was forming a puddle on the floor by her head, collecting in the patchy linoleum next to the table leg. Her right arm was splayed out from her body and he gingerly lifted her wrist, feeling for a pulse. There was nothing.

"Oh, God," he heard himself say. "God, God, God."

No, this wasn't real, this wasn't his life. This was a television show. This was a movie-of-the-week.

Okay. Take a deep breath. Think.

If only I had a cup of strong coffee. Maybe in the cupboard . . .

What, was he crazy? He'd already left fingerprints all over the goddamn place!

Fingerprints!

But, no, wait a minute, she couldn't be dead, that's ridiculous. He could put a mirror in front of her face, see if there was any breath, she had a mirror in her purse. *But that would mean touching more stuff.*

He looked down at the jacket clutched in his hands. It was a mess. One sleeve grazed the spreading puddle of blood. He jerked it up but it was too late. The blood had soaked in.

He'd killed her with a tuxedo.

Art began to laugh, the sound bubbling up inside him and escaping like trapped gas. Tears ran down his cheeks.

But he hadn't meant to kill her at all. The thing to do was call the police and explain what happened.

Oh, yes, wonderful. The police would be very sympathetic down here in the East Village where they were treated like the invading enemy. They'd be real impressed when he told them he was just a tourist from uptown. And when they found the cocaine in her body—and in his body, if they had him checked out—they'd be incredibly understanding.

He went into the bathroom, picked up a hand towel, and wiped every surface he might have touched: the toilet lid, the spigots, the wall by the towel rack.

He found a paper grocery bag folded up next to the garbage can and opened it. He poured his drink down the sink and put the empty glass in the grocery bag, along with the ashtray and its cigarette stubs.

Susan continued to lie there, the blood

slowly trickling toward the door. The apartment's floor was imperceptibly aslant, listing toward the hallway. He'd read somewhere that head wounds bleed the most. He'd have to get out of there before the blood seeped under the door, out into the hall, down the stairs, to the street, snaking and crawling its way like a sticky accusing hand to the nearest police station.

He stuffed the jacket into the bag with the other things.

What else had he touched? Door? He wiped at it. Refrigerator? He couldn't remember, but better wipe it. Light switch? Lamp! Put it back on the table, wipe it down carefully. The photo! For Christ sake, would this ever end?

There was a sound on the street. Sirens!

They knew, they were coming for him! No, don't be crazy, nobody knows. There're always sirens on the street, especially in a neighborhood like this. Wouldn't it be funny if he were mugged after he left?

Take the paper bag. Turn off the lights, using the rag like a glove. Close the door.

Outside the apartment door he heard a sound from downstairs. His heart pounded so loudly it hurt his ears, a desperate *thrump! thrump!* of encased panic. He froze on the stairwell. Please God, don't let them come up here! He heard a door open and shut, the sound of Spanish voices out on the street. More sirens, closer.

Now. Walk casually, don't carry the bag like it's got a bomb in it. Out the front door. Nobody around. Four in the morning.

God, it was cold. And empty. He could be on another planet, the tap-tapping of his hard tight shoes the only sound on the icy street. He walked quickly to Avenue A, a street of metal-shuttered bodegas. First Avenue. He still had the paper bag, he looked just like anyone—in tuxedo pants, no jacket, on an early-winter dawn carrying his groceries home at four in the morning. Just an ordinary pedestrian. Where the hell could he leave it where bums wouldn't rifle through the garbage?

At First Avenue, there were other people on the street, late-night New Wavers in leather and metal leaving the trendy downtown clubs. He was freezing.

A cab stopped at his upraised arm. He gave his address on West Fifty-first Street and leaned back against the taxi seat.

The paper bag tumbled noisily down the dark sooty incinerator shaft in his building. Exhaustion swept over him. And hunger. He changed clothes in his room and went out to an all-night coffee shop on Ninth Avenue. He had taken his first bite of scrambled eggs when he remembered the gift, in its pretty little boutique bag. He'd had it in his jacket pocket. Now it was down the incinerator.

Or was it? He didn't recall feeling its bulge.

It could have fallen out in the apartment. He put his fork down slowly and stared out through the bright fluorescent lights of the coffee shop to a cold, gray dawn.

15

When Margo left the Trump New York Palace Hotel, she was still continuing her argument with Art in her head. How had she ever gotten involved with someone like him? What had she been thinking of? Gregory Sanders was waiting for her outside. He had taken off his glasses and was wiping them with a small cloth.

"Is everything all right?" he asked.

"Oh, yes. Just wonderful. You know, they could have at least *fed* us."

"But I thought you knew it wasn't for dinner."

"That's not the point. The point is that they didn't want to. Just come in, pick up your gold star, and get the hell out!"

"There's no reason to feel mistreated. We knew we were just making an appearance."

"Oh, for heaven's sake," she said. She *had* known that, but what she had really wanted to do was buy a gown and go to the ball like Cinderella. When she got there and saw all those people in their gorgeous clothes, she had been struck with envy. She didn't feel like Margo Magill, representative of the homeless, but more like a child who had her nose pressed to the glass, forbidden to take part in the fun. "I guess I'm just hungry. I get crazy when I'm hungry."

"Do you want to go somewhere?" Gregory asked.

"I don't know."

"He upset you, didn't he?"

"*No.* Yes. A little."

"Is he someone important to you?"

She hesitated. "I was beginning to think so. But now I'm not so sure."

"Well, then. Would you like to go out for a bite to eat? We hardly ever get to really talk."

"That would be nice." She looked around. "Where did Les and Joel go?"

"Home, I think."

"Oh." She felt confused, unable to make a decision.

"Come on, let's go to my place. I'll make us something to eat. Unless you'd rather go to your place?"

"No!"

"What?" he asked.

"Huh?"

"You were smiling. As if you'd just remembered something funny."

"No, no, nothing, just this whole ridiculous night. Your place is fine."

She'd been in Gregory Sanders's apartment once before when he'd given a party for the Coalition staff. She was surprised to find him living in an elegant, high-ceilinged one-bedroom on West Eighty-ninth Street and Riverside Drive, furnished with the touch of a decorator: elegant Empire antiques, several fine Persian rugs, and at least six museum-quality paintings on the walls. Gregory Sanders, she confirmed, came from money. She was always disconcerted to find this out about people she knew. She automatically assumed everyone in her circle was middle-class or below, as she was. When she discovered Gregory's "secret," she became ill at ease around him, alternately fawning and resentful; the way she had felt at the dance, envy warring with disdain.

Gregory didn't seem to notice the change in her, and after a while she began to forgive him for being rich. He was as kind and generous and perfect as he always was, giving enormous energy to the Coalition. Gregory Sanders spent many nights stalking the cold marble halls of Grand Central Station, where hundreds of homeless people huddled on the floors, the benches, and stairs, sneaking into the labyrinthine tunnels where the trains no longer went, and crawling into sooty dark and damp spaces for rest and an illusion of safety. He sought them out, offering food, humane shelter, a kind word.

He had joined other activists in Washington, D.C., in a prolonged hunger strike to protest the closing of a public shelter. After the strike finally succeeded in reopening the shelter, Gregory had returned to New York forty pounds thinner, but triumphant. Margo was impressed, although a cynical voice inside her said that Gregory Sanders just felt guilty about growing up rich and was turning his life into one long atonement.

Gregory took Margo's coat and hung it in the foyer closet. This time, without other people to distract her, she was able to explore the apartment while he went into the kitchen. She was drawn to one dramatically beautiful landscape painting over the sofa in the living room, a waterfall done in brilliant hues of blue. The water seemed to leap from the canvas into the room.

Gregory entered, holding two glasses of white wine in generous goblets. He handed her one and went back into the kitchen for a plate of cheese, crackers, and fruit.

"I hope this is enough," he said.

"It looks great. And that painting is . . . amazing."

"I know. It's a Bierstadt. My great-grandfather bought it when the artist was alive. I love the whole realistic school of art. I'm old-fashioned, I guess. I like landscapes, portraits, things that look like things, people's faces. . . ."

He trailed off, took a sip of wine, still regarding the painting.

"So do I," she said. "I look at most modern art and I think, Well, that's interesting, I wonder what it is I'm supposed to feel. Once an artist told me that my bewilderment was as important a response as any other and I believed him for a while. I was much younger then and we were going out, so . . ." She shrugged and laughed. "So I'd wander around the SoHo galleries with him looking at canvases painted all white, with maybe a spot in one corner, or all shades of stripes or looking like mud, or just a mess of color like some kid had gotten into the finger paints, and I'd nod and smile and say, 'Fascinating! Look what he's done with negative space!' Until I realized that I was confusing bewilderment with boredom."

"I have a Milton Resnick in the bedroom. I guess I won't show it to you," Gregory said with a smile. She didn't reply, hoping he wouldn't notice she wasn't familiar with the artist's name.

"Jackson Pollock school," he added.

"Yes, of course." Why didn't she *know* these things? She really should take some night classes, fill in her cultural gaps. She'd been planning to register for some courses at the New School, but then Art had come along, absorbing her nights, her spare hours. Well, that was over. Now she'd have plenty of free time. She spread some Brie on a cracker, topped it with a slice of apple, and took a bite. It was delicious. She really was hungry.

"Is that going to be enough? I could heat up some soup. Or make you a sandwich. I like to cook but I never seem to have the time, so I don't keep much around." Gregory reached over and wiped off a minute crumb that had dropped from the cracker to the coffee table.

"Oh, this will be fine." She ate some more. "But they really *could* have given us dinner," she said.

"I think that was my fault. I've been to so many of those things, I guess it never occurred to me that anyone would find them interesting. I thought we'd want to get in and out fast, not hang around having to, uh, schmooze."

She laughed at his self-conscious use of the Yiddish word. She had been taught a lot of Jewish slang by Michael, who couldn't keep a straight face when she kept repeating "kvetch" as if it had two syllables. "Not 'ka-vetch'!" he'd correct her, breaking up. "*Kvetch!*"

"I'll put on some music," Gregory said. "Unless you'd rather talk without it." He was looking at her in a new way, or at least one she'd never noticed before. When their eyes met, he blinked slightly and she could see a tightening in his jaw.

He wanted to sleep with her, she realized. Funny she had never noticed before. She was usually pretty attuned to these things, but she had always thought of Gregory as monklike.

Certainly he was handsome, in a slightly bland way, all even features and straight sandy hair combed back from his forehead; tortoise shell glasses which he often removed when he was ill at ease. He was doing it now.

"So, Margo, what do you do in your spare time?"

"What spare time?"

"Maybe we could play some tennis sometime. Or go skiing this winter."

"I've never skiied, I'm afraid. And I don't play tennis very well. But when do *you* find the time, with all the stuff you do?"

He brightened, as if he had been waiting for her to ask that very question. "Ah! Organization! That's the secret. We can do anything we want if we know how to budget time."

Why did she have the feeling she was in a seminar?

"Yes, I try, but between my work at the hospital and the clinic and the shelter and the streets, there isn't much left." And fucking Art takes up a lot of time, too, she thought, but didn't say. "And it seems whenever I push myself too hard, I get a cold or flu or something. I'm one of those people who needs food and sleep, I'm afraid."

"Illness is only something you create out of negative energy. I never get sick, because I refuse to let in those thoughts that would compromise my immune system. I can't allow it. I have too much to do."

Margo started to speak up, but stopped. She wanted to tell him that she thought that kind of reasoning was mostly a smug crock of shit, from people who thought they could control everything, even their own mortality.

Instead, she tried to concentrate on Gregory's fine features and clear blue eyes and what was obviously a trim body underneath his clothes. If he would just shut up, they could make love and then everything would be fine.

"I might like to see that painting in the bedroom." She smiled slyly.

"Really?" He seemed genuinely surprised and for a second she thought she had been too aggressive, that she had read him wrong and he wasn't really interested in her at all. Maybe he was one of those New Celibates that get written up in *New York* magazine articles.

"Well, then, let me just get these things into the kitchen," he said, picking up the food and dishes.

"I think they can wait," she suggested.

"Oh, no, not in this city. I don't want cockroaches."

He carefully carried the plates and glasses away and she could hear him running the water in the kitchen sink.

Was he actually doing the dishes now?

Margo sighed and wandered over to Gregory's desk. There was a tidy stack of papers, two pens, and two sharpened pencils standing up in a silver holder; a daily calendar with a list of things to do in a small, deliberate print, each accomplished item checked off. His computer loomed over the desk, its screen blank. She opened one of the small drawers and saw stamps, Whiteout, and staples, all neatly arranged. She slid the drawer closed, feeling a little dizzy.

"Well, all done," he said, coming up behind her. He was holding two more glasses of wine.

"This is a zinfandel," he said solemnly.

Margo had lost her initial flush of desire by the time he set his wine down on the coffee table and pulled her to him. He kissed her for a long time, slowly and sensually, running his hands down her back. He kissed very well, and after a while she was able to relax into it.

When she opened her eyes, she saw the beautiful painting over his shoulder. She liked the idea of herself in this gracious apartment, warmed by the wine and Gregory Sanders's body.

If only Art were here so that she could show him the painting, lead him around the apartment, saying, look at this, and this, and this!

Annoyed by the direction of her thoughts, she put her attention on Gregory, kissing him deeply. She slid her hand up behind his head to grasp the base of his neck, the way Art liked—

No, that wasn't what she should be thinking. Think about Gregory. She followed him into the bedroom noticing first the large abstract canvas on the wall over the bed.

She thought of that time in her apartment when she and Art had come back from a long afternoon of squabbling and hurting each other, finally drawn into a ritual of forgiveness, restating their feelings over and over. She couldn't get enough of him that day. Other days. He had made her insatiable, she who had easily relegated sex to a small corner of her life, somewhere below chocolate and television. Her grinding impatience as he undressed her, and each time she could hardly wait to take him in her hand, in her mouth, there was something about the taste of him that she couldn't get enough of. Was there some mingling of chemicals between certain people that created a perfect combination? Because she had never felt so connected to any man as she did to Art.

And now a different man was undressing her, touching her. Her body went about its business of responding, but it was a technical performance. She had to concentrate hard on erotic fantasies, slipping them into the video-cassette player in her mind. When one didn't work, she tried another, each more outrageous than the last: bondage; S&M; harem slaves, masked, oiled black men. She passed images before her mind's eye, straining for arousal and escape from the truth that she was as close as a person could get to a man she didn't love, didn't desire, except as a brief respite from reality. And that there was a man out there she did love, and yet she felt compelled to drive him away, to hurt him. As Gregory pumped away in her body, she thought of Art's baleful expression when she'd left him a few hours earlier, and she knew that no matter how hard she tried, or Gregory tried, or how many visions she conjured up, this just would not work.

I haven't faked it in years, she thought, looking at herself in the bathroom mirror a little while later. But she felt she owed it to Gregory, who had tried so hard and clearly cared for her. Just the sort of man a woman would want. Only she didn't.

She left quickly, making up a story about having forgotten to feed her neighbor's cat. Gregory insisted on throwing on his clothes and seeing her into a cab. It was nearly four in the morning when she kissed him good-bye, and he told her he'd call her later in the day. Riding home in the cab, she felt ashamed of her own dishonesty. What had she been trying to prove? Whatever it was, it hadn't been worth using Gregory Sanders.

She didn't even take off her coat but went straight to the telephone. The blinking light of her answering machine caught her eye and she played back the night's one message. She laughed aloud with relief when she heard Art's voice going on and on. Before it was through, she was dialing Jack's, but there was no answer. She searched through a pile of papers for the number of Art's latest residence.

"Washington Irving Hotel," said a bored Hispanic male voice.

"Could you ring Art Glenn's room please?"

It rang. And rang. And rang. After a long time the receptionist came back on the phone.

"He ain't there. You wanna leave a message?"

"No. No message."

She put down the phone, disappointed. So. Nothing had changed. He was probably out with somebody else. Maybe that little debutante in the red dress. What had she been thinking of? He was a tomcat. A wharf rat. A stray. The best thing she could do would be to forget about him and get on with her life.

It was already dawn, a time of day that made her uneasy, as if she were doing something illicit simply by being awake. She turned on the television, flipped through the channels with the remote. She stared at MTV for a few minutes, the gyrating figures on the screen a meaningless blur.

16

He stood before a small, weathered cabin at the edge of a river. The water rushed by in a furious roar of sound. In his right hand he carried a shopping bag. He stepped onto the cabin's crumbling porch, the boards creaking beneath his feet, and entered through a door that hung on by only one hinge. At first it was hard to see in the cabin's gloomy interior, but as his eyes adjusted he was able to make out the shapes of decaying furniture, layered with dust and cobwebs. He swallowed, filled with an unnamed terror.

"Did you bring it?" a voice said.

The man was sitting on a rocking chair, and somehow Art had not noticed him when he came in, or heard the distinct rasp of the rocker on the gritty floor.

"Yes. I brought what I could."

"Good." The man got to his feet with some effort and went to a small refrigerator. He opened it, the light bulb inside casting a dusty beam across the room. He held his hand out for the shopping bag and Art gave it to him. "We're running low," said the man.

Art stepped closer so that he could see inside the refrigerator.

It was filled with human body parts, some wrapped in butcher paper, most loose and bloody. Hands. Thighs. Necks. Ankles. Testicles. Breasts. Livers.

The man nonchalantly removed more parts from the bag Art had brought, humming to himself a tune that Art could just barely make out: ". . . I love all of you. . . ."

Art felt panic slam into him and he backed up, a scream filling his throat. He couldn't find the doorknob in the dim light and fumbled in terror trying to escape. He heard a thunk as something in the man's hand fell to the floor, and he heard himself screaming "Let me out," and another thunk, and another.

Someone was knocking at the door.

"Ay! You in there? Ay, you, Glenn!"

Bam! bam! bam! went a fist on the door.

He leaped from the bed, still half-lost in the nightmare.

"Yes, I'm here, just a second." He was nude. A pair of his dirty underpants lay on the floor and he pulled them on and then his jeans, and unlocked the door.

The hotel manager was leaning against the door frame.

"You owe for the rent. Last week. Guy at the desk say you been slipping out so he don't see you. No rent, no room. Okay?"

"Yeah, sure. Listen, I got it. I got a check right here, I'll get it cashed, okay?"

"It's Friday night already."

"Oh, yeah, right. Well, tomorrow, then. A friend of mine'll cash it."

The guy shook his head wearily: he'd been through this before. "Guess I don't have no choice. Right?"

Art smiled. "Right!" The man didn't smile back.

"And hey, you been gettin' some calls, but the desk couldn't put 'em through cause your line's been busy all day."

"Busy?" He looked for the phone, which was half under the bed, its receiver off the hook. He reached down and replaced it. "Oh, uh, you can put the calls through now. I must've knocked it off. Sorry."

"Ain't my calls." The manager walked back down the hall.

Art's hands were shaking, a combination of hangover and fear. That dream! But it had only been a dream, and it would fade, it would.

Susan.

"Oh, shit." That part was real.

Art checked his watch, lying on the night table: 4:45. He had slept all day. His room faced an air shaft, so there was very little indication of night or day. He switched on the light and looked around at the disheveled bed, the small table, ashtrays spilling over with old, foul-smelling butts, one shabby chair next to a sooty window. He remembered the dance, the van Dessings. What would they make of him if they saw this?

He picked up the phone and called his service. Charlotte van Dessing's social secretary had called twice. Perhaps they had underpaid him. Or had paid him too much and wanted it back. The way things were going, that was more likely.

"Oh, Mr. Glenn!" said the secretary when he called back. "I'm so glad I caught you before Charlotte left town. She's flying to Florida tonight and wanted to know if you might be available to play on the yacht, and at the resort."

"Excuse me?"

"Oh, I'm sorry, let me backtrack. Charlotte—Mrs. van Dessing—and some friends—and her daughter, I think—are taking the boat to the islands. It's a lovely yacht and it has a beautiful piano, and Char—Mrs. van Dessing thought you might be just perfect to play. She'll pay generously, of course, and you'll have a little trip for yourself. They're going to the Elation Island Surf Club, do you know it?"

"No."

"Oh, well, it's lovely. And Charlotte says she's sure they'd pay you to play at the hotel—if you want to, that is. Or you could take a flight home at that point. It's up to you. But I'm afraid it's very short notice. You'd have to be ready to leave tonight."

He looked around the room. Leave all this? He could barely keep the urgency from his voice, forced himself to sound calm and blasé.

"It sounds . . . good. Real good. But I have to work out a few things."

"Certainly. Do you want to call back when you're sure? It's just that I'd have to get you on a flight."

"No, no, I was just really . . . thinking out loud. I can go, definitely. But, uh, this may sound silly, but my tux got a little, uh, messed up. I, uh, fell last night coming home, and it will have to go to the cleaners."

"I'm sorry, are you all right?"

"Yes, yes, I'm fine."

"You'd really be better off with a white jacket anyway, for the tropics."

"Sure, right."

"Then you'll be available?"

"Well, yes, I guess so. Yes!"

He wrote down the airline information. After hanging up, he left a message on Mattie Greene's answering machine, asking him to continue to sub, then called Jack, who agreed to cash his check.

Art showered quickly in the cruddy bathroom down the hall and shaved carefully. Back in his room, he packed up most of his possessions in one large suitcase, wondering if he could get out of the hotel without attracting notice. If the manager weren't around, then maybe . . .

He put a few clothes and toilet articles into a smaller bag, hanging his only lightweight pale yellow jacket and a creased pair of white slacks in a garment carrier. He would stash the rest of his stuff in Jack's storeroom.

His head reeling, still groggy from sleep and the nightmare, from too little food and too much substance abuse, he left the hotel with his bags. The desk clerk, nodding over the sports pages of the *New York Post*, didn't notice Art as he exited, but it wasn't until he was a block away and getting into a cab that Art was able to take a deep breath and allow himself a moment of triumph.

17

The yacht plowed south into blue glassy waters. Art leaned against the rail, breathing in the tangy salt air. With each mile that passed, he felt the mess of his life receding into the distance. He was really very lucky, he thought, it was kind of uncanny how lucky he was. If only he could get rid of the anxiety that was rolled into a tiny hard ball deep in his gut. He took in a cleansing breath of sea air, and for a moment the panic was replaced by a surge of elation. Yes, Art Glenn had landed on his feet again.

"Good morning. Nearly afternoon, really," said Jinx, coming out onto the deck. She was wearing a tiny aqua bikini with a sheer matching sheath over it. She held a mug of steaming coffee. "I didn't hear you get up."

"Afternoon," he said, turning away from her look, which presumed a certain degree of intimacy, now that they'd made love, if that was what it was called. Somehow, he didn't even remember how he'd ended up in bed with Jinx last night.

Art tapped a Marlboro from his pack and cupped his hand to shield the match from the wind as he lit the cigarette.

"Nicotine," Jinx said with an envious sigh. He handed the lit cigarette to her and took out another for himself. She inhaled and blew the smoke into the wind. "We're nearly there. We're nearly to the islands."

He could just make out a patch of green on the horizon, a lightening of the water to a paler blue. The gentle, relentless pitching of the boat tormented his hangover and he welcomed the thought of firm land beneath his feet.

It had been a long night. He'd had too many drinks on the plane—flying always frightened him—and by the time they'd landed and been driven to the boat, it was after midnight.

Jinx had insisted on taking him on a quick tour of the yacht's interior. She carried a bottle of vintage Taittinger in her left hand, gripping Art's arm with her right. He didn't even like champagne, it gave him a headache.

"Do you know much about boats?" she asked.

"They float."

"Terrific. I'll start at the beginning."

"Is there a bottle of whiskey somewhere on it?"

"Probably."

"And a piano?"

"Of course."

"Well, that's all I need to know."

"Come on, this is for your own good."

"I prefer things that are bad for me."

"Do you?"

"Uh-huh."

"I'm sure you'll find plenty of that tonight."

"I usually do."

She laughed and took a swig from the bottle, offered it to him. He sipped and made a face. "The bubbles tickle my nose," he said soberly.

Jinx looked quite different in the preppy white boat clothes she'd changed into. Her behind and thighs were still a little too plump for his taste, but there was an agreeable and old-fashioned symmetry to her body, generous bosom and hips divided by a tiny waist. She pulled him by the hand, taking on the role of tour guide. "This is a Broward yacht, a hundred and forty feet long, really just a small one."

"A rowboat."

"No, really. Compared to some of Mama's friends. And the Arabs? Unreal. Some Arab prince was in Palm Beach last winter and he threw a big party. There were wives in chadors all over the place and he had a plate of cocaine like *this*." She held her hands a foot apart.

She showed him the main deck with its well-stocked bar. They passed through the adjacent large dining room and walked through to the lounge, where a gleaming black baby grand piano stood in one corner. "I think Mama had it tuned recently, so it should be pretty good," Jinx said. "And it's just for tonight. Tomorrow we'll be at the island."

"Where is it we're going again?" he asked, looking back at the bar as they left.

"Elation Island. It's great. You'll see. I'll let Randall tell you about it, he loves to go on and on about island lore."

"Randall?"

"He's my very good friend who was at the dance. Tall and thin? Well, you'll meet him soon enough. He's aboard already."

She led him through the kitchen—the galley—informing him that there was another, smaller galley on the lower deck, used by the crew. Art hoped the tour would be over soon and he could sit down, but Jinx led him up a short staircase to the master stateroom. Charlotte was just coming out, changed into white slacks and a gray linen blouse. She invited them in to look around, pointing out the pale blues and peach and white that a decorator had blended harmoniously in the suite. "Aren't the colors lovely?" she cooed.

"Yes, they're all my favorites," he said, noticing the king-size bed and the large circular Jacuzzi.

"My daughter giving you the guided tour?" she asked.

"Like a pro," he replied, thinking that it came out sounding wrong.

Down the hall were two other staterooms. "This is yours," Jinx said, leading him into the room. It was as large as a hotel suite, with a picture window that faced the water, and it was certainly bigger than most of his many apartments.

"Is it all right?" she asked, misinterpreting his frown.

"I think it will do." He left his bags next to the bed.

Downstairs a glass-enclosed area led to the upper sunning deck, cocktail lounge, and the pilothouse. Jinx quickly introduced Art to the pilot, who smoked a pipe and nodded a greeting, and the co-pilot, a young sun-blond beach god.

On they went, to see three more staterooms on the level below, each with private bath, queen-size beds, stereo system, and wide views of the water. "And here's the sauna," she said, indicating a closed wooden room. "The crew—there's four of them, they sleep downstairs. And the rest of the staff, too." She gestured vaguely aft.

Art was thoroughly confused by the time they got back to the lounge, where the guests were gathering. He felt as if he'd been blindfolded and spun around and now was supposed to perform some clever feat no one had explained to him.

The room was lively with chatter and the clinking of drinks. He approached the bar and asked the bartender for a Jack Daniel's on the rocks. After the first sip, he paused for a sigh of gratitude, to the whiskey gods, to his own personal benefactor wherever and whatever it was, and downed the rest in one long swallow. He asked for a double and took it with him to the piano.

There were eight or ten people in the room, but the only ones Art recognized from the Sweethearts' Ball were Charlotte's boyfriend Bittles, and Randall, whom Jinx brought over to introduce to Art. "My dear, dear friend Randall Woods Prentice. And this is our fabulous piano player, Art Glenn."

"I enjoy your playing," Randall said, shaking Art's hand. Art liked him immediately.

Randall's tall, thin frame was set off by safari shorts, exposing tanned, golden-haired legs. He wore a black Polo knit shirt and white topsiders. A Panama hat tilted over his face, shadowing intense blue eyes. Randall just missed being truly good-looking, his shoulders too thin and narrow, his facial planes severe and appearing almost fleshless. Art wondered how old he was. He looked anywhere between thirty and fifty.

"Art Glenn," Randall repeated. "I knew a Jennifer Glenn at school. She was from Philadelphia."

"No relation that I know of," Art said pleasantly.

"Where *are* your people from?" Jinx asked him.

"All over. The Bronx, Brooklyn, Cleveland."

Jinx stared, then burst out laughing. "Oh!" she said, as if she'd just gotten the joke. She pulled Randall's hat off and put it on her own head. He grabbed it back playfully and they passed it back and forth until Randall prevailed and planted the hat firmly back on his head. Art looked from one to the other, laughing along because it seemed like the proper response.

"Is Maria cooking?" Randall asked Jinx when they calmed down. "I'm ravenous."

"No, darn it, she had some family crisis in Bogotá, so we've got Kim, the Benders' girl."

"Oh, yes, she's good, but not as good as Maria."

"*No* one's as good as Maria. And I thought we could do a barbecue on the beach."

"Only if *you* don't cook," Randall teased. He looked at Art for moral support. "The last barbecue, we went to some tiny island, practically a sandbar, and we hauled all this stuff off the boat for a cookout—why we couldn't stay on the boat I have no idea."

"Atmosphere."

"Atmosphere, all right. There were about a million sand flies and they ate more of us than we did of those burned steaks."

"Oh, you were too blasted to know the difference." She turned to Art. "He'd already complained that I'd only brought meat and he was a vegetarian all of a sudden. Are you still?"

"No, I'm eating corpse again, it was just too boring without it."

"Oh, Ran!" she exclaimed, poking him in the arm. He poked her back and he grabbed her hand and engaged her in an intense game of thumb wrestling. When Randall won, Jinx squealed and looked at Art and rolled her eyes. "Isn't he the most outrageous person you've ever seen?"

Art nodded and smiled and tried to look interested. Then he excused himself and went to the piano, grateful to have the music to escape into, even if no one was listening.

He entertained till three, while the yacht *Charlotte's Web* slipped quietly from her berth in Port Everglades. He hadn't even noticed they were out on the ocean until he stopped playing and walked out on deck, into a night of hazy stars and churning black water. He could see the party continuing behind the sliding glass doors, the soundless laughter and movement choreographed like some strange dance, people costumed in cool white, interspersed now and then by a patch of color, a pastel, a flash of bright jewelry. They were not real to him but seemed to be playing on a television screen with the sound muted.

A wave of isolation came over him and he turned to watch the sea. All at once he was twenty-five again, far out in the ocean, climbing to the top of the ocean liner's smokestack in the middle of the night with his stupid stoned pals, daring the wind to carry him away. The fear came tearing into him, the memory of how close he had been to death, and he thought that drowning would be the most terrifying death of all. But of course he hadn't died that night on the ocean liner and he was not about to die now. Why did he have to be so morbid just when things were going his way again?

He went back inside for another drink.

Late, very late, the cook Kim brought out platters of food: conch salad, peas and rice, cold crabmeat and lobster on shaved ice, sapodilla ice cream. They ate buffet style in the spacious lounge, from delicate china plates, but Art had little appetite. The food was beautiful and alien, tasteless in his mouth, an assortment of textures. He put the plate down on a table and crossed quickly to the other side of the room, as if he had done something dirty.

"Oh, I love staying up all night!" said Jinx. 'It's just like school!"

"Peter told me the headwinds will slow us down," Bittles remarked, referring to the boat's captain. "We won't get to the island till late morning."

"I think I'll turn in," said Charlotte, covering a yawn. "Bit?"

"I'll be along in a few minutes. I hope we don't get a storm. Maybe I should check with Peter."

"I don't care," said Jinx. "I could stay out here forever." She walked to the glass door that opened onto the deck. "Sometimes I think I was a sea creature in another life."

"A blowfish," said Randall dryly.

"Very funny. No, a dolphin. Or a mermaid."

"I think that's merperson."

Bittles excused himself, leaving only Randall, Art, Jinx, and Leila and Yves, a quiet French couple in their early twenties Jinx had met at an after-hours club a few weeks before.

"What are the lives you've never lived?" Randall said suddenly to Art, who had discovered a cache of sheet music in the piano bench and was looking through it.

"I don't know what you mean."

"Well, Jinx—like the estimable Shirley MacLaine—thinks she's lived before in other forms. Me, I only have lives I *wish* I'd lived. What about you? If you could do it all again, who would you be?"

"Well, uh . . . I don't know. Is it too late?" Art laughed shortly.

"Of course!" said Randall.

"Ran, you're *so* negaholic," Jinx snapped.

"How old are you Art?"

"Uh. Thirty," he lied.

"Thirty years. Gone."

"This is depressing, Ran, leave him alone."

Yves spoke up. "You play for us again? The piano?"

"Sure—"

"For example," Randall continued, as if no one else had spoken, "I always wanted to be a

SEAL. S-E-A-L. Sea-Air-Land. That's the military demolition corps that do all kinds of dangerous nasty things, like sabotaging foreign ships."

"Why?" Jinx asked.

"For wars. And intelligence."

"What's the point?" Jinx said airily. "Now *I'd* like to have been a flight nurse in Vietnam. I read a book about these nurses and how they took the injured soldiers on the plane and they'd try to save their lives using whatever medicine was at hand and sometimes they'd run out."

"*You'd* never run out. I can just see it, some poor GI dying of shrapnel wounds and Jinx, in her little white nurse costume, would offer him a snort."

Yves spoke up. "I like to be a . . ." He struggled for the English. "Archeologue . . ."

"Archaeologist," said Randall.

"Yes."

"So be one, you're young yet. *Tu est très jeune.*"

Yves shrugged, smiled sunnily. "*Non, non.* I am . . . *trop indolent.*"

"He's too lazy," translated Jinx, for Art's benefit.

"Hey, I know French!" Art cracked. "I've sung Jacques Brel!"

"Jacques Brel?" Leila perked up. "*J'aime les chansons de Brel!*" She asked him to sing some and all at once everyone was clustered around the piano. Art felt the line blur between being a hired musician and a member of the party. He tried to calculate how many hours he'd been playing and wondered if he would be paid extra.

*"Oh, mon amour, mon doux, mon tendre, mon
    merveilleux amour
De l'aube clair jusqu'à la fin du jour
Je t'aime encore, tu sais
Je t'aime. . . ."*

Leila was crying when he finished the song. She laughed and wiped her eyes on the back of her hand. Yves leaned over and kissed her on each cheek. Art was reminded of Margo, who was so easily moved by sentiment she cried at the opening credits of movies. His thoughts jumped from Margo to the dance and their last words, to the body in the apartment, an image he had tried to drive from his mind. He turned to the piano and began to play the first thing that came to him. He was horrified to hear himself pound out the melody to "Don't Cry Out Loud." He stopped.

"Oh, I like that song!" said Jinx.

He was about to relate his list of songs he never played when the blond Adonis co-pilot came into the lounge and gave them a late update on the weather and their progress.

"Are we lost at sea?" Jinx asked him flirtatiously. Art saw her sit up a little straighter, self-consciously playing with a strand of hair.

"No, Miss Jinx, we're right on course," he replied, looking from her to Randall, who smiled and put his arm around the co-pilot's shoulder. Jinx frowned.

"Tell me—Jimmy?"

"Gibby."

"Ah, yes, Gibby. What would you have done with your life if you didn't work on boats?"

Gibby shrugged. "I guess I'd like to be a dog trainer."

Jinx laughed sharply, with a disdainful edge. The co-pilot blushed, his tanned face turning rosy under his yellow-white hair.

Randall said, "Now come on, that sounds perfectly respectable to me."

"I meant, you know, seeing-eye dogs. Police dogs."

"Oh," she said, "I thought you meant those little poodles in funny hats that stand on their hind feet." She laughed again, shrilly.

Yves and Leila conversed in French, trying to understand what was so amusing. Randall offered Gibby a drink but he declined and quickly excused himself. Randall stared at the empty door when Gibby had gone.

"Actually," Randall said after a moment, "*I* would like to arrange my own kidnapping, then drop from sight for several years, have myself declared dead, and come back in disguise for my own funeral. Eavesdrop on what everybody really thinks of me. Surprise!"

There was a pause, the only sounds the hum

of the boat's engines far below, the splash of water, and the tick of the stately grandfather clock in the room. Art thought that that was a wonderful idea, the way to really start over and still get to see how it all turned out.

"Really, Randall," said Jinx.

Leila whispered to Yves, *"Enlever,"* and he frowned.

"I was only joking," said Randall.

"Some things aren't funny. Mama's already paranoid enough, she won't go anywhere without her bodyguard, she practically takes him into the bathroom with her. I wouldn't let her hire one for me."

"Jinx, let's face it, Charlotte *likes* having that hunk go everywhere she goes. And frankly I don't blame her."

"That's not nice, even if it is true. Should we open another bottle of the Taittinger? Where's the bartender? Where's Kim? Oh, rats, everyone's gone to sleep? I'll get it myself. Anyone else?"

"You wouldn't happen to have another bottle of Jack Daniel's around, would you?" Art asked.

"Ah, the old friend Jack," said Randall. "I'll have a shot of that, too. Enough of this carbonated piss. Unless you have some magic white powder."

"It's too late for that tonight," said Jinx primly.

"Says you. What are you, the substance monitor?"

"For heaven's sake." Jinx went off and presently returned with an armful of liquor bottles and a little vial of cocaine. Randall poured shots for himself and Art. Jinx laid out lines on a hand mirror and passed it around, with a rolled twenty-dollar bill. Art felt the jolt of the drug, the pleasant bitter sting at the back of his throat, and a sense of magnanimous well-being. The night was extraordinarily beautiful and his shadowy panic vanished. The conversation hummed along like a background accompaniment, serving much the same purpose his playing did at a party.

"I want to be a movie star," said Leila shyly.

"*Poof!* You're a movie star!" Randall declared. "Look, darling, you and Jinx aren't old enough to enter into this discussion. You have to live long enough to have some serious regrets. At least to age twenty-three."

"She could be a film star," said Jinx, reaching over to touch Leila's long silky black hair. "She should model."

"In Maroc, the magazine *Elle* took photos. Not many clothing. My father, he was vairy pissed off."

The others laughed at her choice of words and accent.

For a while everyone was quiet, the only sound coming from the low hum of the boat's engines. Art closed his eyes, the humming noise turning into a whine, then a cry of pain that went on and on. He shook his head, to dispel the sensation. The quick high of the coke had topped off in only a few moments. He looked at the empty vial lying on the coffee table and was irritated with Jinx for bringing so little.

"Are we there yet?" said Jinx playfully, breaking the silence.

"Where exactly is 'there'?" Art asked.

"Oh, yes, Ran, I promised you'd tell Art all about Elation."

"We're getting near the Bahamas by now, I'd guess," Randall replied. He took a large atlas from the bookshelf and leafed through to find the Caribbean. "There. Nassau. Eleuthera over there, those little dots are Harbour Island and Spanish Wells. There's Cat Island, and down here, farther south and east—right there—Elation Island. It's not marked well on this map, don't you have a more detailed one?"

"Maybe Mama would, but she's asleep."

"Well, this will do. You can see the island is fairly isolated, away from the cluster, which is the reason it has such an odd history."

"There are cats on Cat Island?" Leila asked.

"A few, but no more than normal. But there are dogs on Elation. In fact—"

"Dogs?" Art interrupted.

"Yes, dogs; in fact, that's how it got its name: Les Chiens. It was named by the French. Later, English pirates came along and bastardized the name."

Jinx remarked, "Is he going off on those pirates again? Every time we come down here, he's off about the pirates."

"Maybe it's a life I missed."

"There were women pirates, too," said Jinx. "I read a book about them. Anne Bonny. Mary Read. They sailed with Calico Jack and they disguised themselves as men."

"It's called drag now, honey, and it was drag then."

"Can you imagine trying to pass yourself off as a man on one of those cramped little sailing ships? All that time at sea, never going to the bathroom in front of anyone? With those sailors probably comparing whose is bigger and seeing who can pee further over the side?"

"Boys will be boys," Randall commented.

"And what about when the women got their periods? There sure wasn't Tampax then, all those bloody rags."

"Must we?"

"Oh, don't get all squeamish, Ran. I remember that dinner party—at the Breakers, for goodness' sake—when you launched into a detailed description of intestinal parasites and how one gets them."

"That was instructional, my dear. A stitch in time—"

"Is worth two in the bush," she finished.

"Why are there a lot of dogs?" asked Art, a hard ball of fear beginning to swell again and press against his insides.

"Ah! That goes back to the legend of the first

settlers." Randall picked up his glass. "Let's go out on deck and watch the dawn come up."

With some grumbling, they carried cups and glasses, plates of food, liquor bottles, and several blankets to keep off the damp late-night chill. Art settled into a lounge chair, rocking back until he was looking straight up at an alarming array of stars.

There was not yet a hint of light in the sky, but as Randall told his story, the horizon began to pale to slate, then a lighter gray, and finally, the orange rim of the rising sun coated the water with a shimmering layer of silver and gold.

The sea slapped the sides of the moving boat and from far away came a lonely hoot that could be a bird or a distant ship.

18

"Two hundred and seventy-five years ago, on the rocky coast of Brittany, a French landowner's young son fell in love with a peasant's daughter."

Jinx interrupted. "That's not the way you told it last time."

"Yes, it is," Randall replied. "And give me a refill, I need fuel."

Jinx took the bottle of whiskey from Art and passed it over to Randall.

"As I was saying, these two young people fell in love. They lived in a small village at the very tip of the Brittany peninsula, where the winds are wild and the sea crashes against the land so hard that in the old days, people feared their little peninsula might break off and float out to sea. That was before they understood the nature of geological formations and still believed in sea dragons."

"You mean there aren't sea dragons?" Jinx remarked.

"Ssh. Now, the young man—Jacques—lived in a large and luxurious stone mansion, while the young woman—Marie—lived in a crude, damp, peat-roofed shack with her father. Marie's mother had died giving birth to her and her father often drank to drown his sorrow and loneliness. He loved his daughter but she so resembled her mother that every time he looked at her, he was painfully reminded of what he had lost.

"At fifteen, she was even more beautiful than her mother had been. She had masses of golden hair that fell in cascading ringlets down her back all the way to her waist. Her eyes were the gray green of the sea on a stormy day, her skin as pale as the inside of a delicate shell.

"One day, Jacques, who at sixteen was a tall, strapping lad with fiery red hair from his Celtic ancestors, came into the village to buy some goats. He saw Marie trying in vain to sell a basketful of wild pink roses that had sprung up almost magically in her little garden. Jacques was so entranced, he bought all her flowers for a very generous price indeed.

"For days after, he couldn't get the beautiful peasant girl out of his mind. Marie had not been able to forget the handsome young man who bought her flowers either, but she knew that her father wanted her to enter the convent. They began to meet in secret, in a secluded spot that looked onto the ocean, and they fell so deeply in love they could not imagine living without each other. Jacques vowed that he would tell his father that he wanted to marry Marie.

"But Jacques's father only laughed at his foolish son's notion of marrying a peasant girl. He had planned for Jacques to marry the plump, stupid daughter of the Marquis de Régine. If Jacques refused, and persisted in this crazy infatuation, he would be disinherited.

"Each night, after slipping off to see Marie for a few blissful, stolen moments, Jacques walked along the rocky shore on the rich black sand. He thought more and more of leaving his home and taking Marie to a faraway place. He noticed a merchant galleon sailing into the port at St. Nazaire, and all at once he knew what they must do.

"He stole a bag of gold coins from his father's secret stash to buy them passage on the next merchant vessel going to the New World. Marie was frightened but knew if she wanted to be with Jacques, she had no choice."

Randall paused in his storytelling, took a long drink from his glass, and stretched his body before resuming. The others waited in silence. Art concentrated on one particular star high up in the sky, a sense of foreboding growing inside him.

"Jacques's gold coins easily purchased two passages on the creaky *L'Etoile de la Mer.* Before dawn on the morning they were to sail, both lovers slipped out of their homes for the last time, carrying what few possessions they could, and met on the outskirts of the village. Marie had brought a small burlap bag containing her few clothes and a Bible. Trailing behind her on a rope leash was her shaggy white dog, Belle, an odd cross of foxhound and Belgian sheepdog.

"Jacques was stunned. 'They won't allow a dog aboard!' he cried. But Marie was adamant, and eventually Jacques relented, promising to pay whatever was needed to include Belle as a passenger.

"It was then that Jacques took out his knife and chopped off lock after lock of Marie's hair because it was necessary for her to disguise herself as a man in order to be allowed on the ship. The gold ringlets fell to the ground, and they left them there. She put on Jacques's cap and an old jacket and breeches he had brought, and the transformation was complete.

"Once aboard, the captain's palm filled with extra gold to allow the canine passenger, the young lovers endured a long, hard voyage, filled with sickness and strife among the crew, who were a seedy, rough bunch. Marie lived in dread of being discovered to be a female. Jacques worried that while they slept, some wretched sailor would kill them and steal his remaining gold. It also became increasingly clear that Belle was expecting a litter of puppies, and Marie feared that the crew would toss them overboard, or eat them.

"The ship was still a great distance from the port at Charleston when a huge storm blew up. The captain and crew fought mightily to keep control of the ship, but the fierce winds ripped the sails to shreds. A mast came crashing down onto the deck. Water flooded the ship from top to bottom, while the storm continued to howl all around them.

"Jacques and Marie huddled below, sick and frightened. All at once there was a pounding on their door. 'Abandon ship!' a sailor cried. 'We're going down!' They could barely make their way up to the deck. The sea was already claiming *L'Etoile de la Mer* and all it carried. Sailors, cargo, captain, sails, dog, masts, all were swept overboard into the roiling sea. Marie and Jacques held on to one another for as long as they could, but the surging water wrenched them apart and sent them floating, flotsam and jetsam, on the merciless waves.

"Jacques had little memory of the next hours, or days, or moments, for there was no way for him to tell how much time passed. He felt himself going under for the last time and was beginning to welcome the peace that might come with death, when he felt a strange and buoyant lift beneath his tired body. A sea creature, long and silver gray, with a face that seemed to smile, was carrying him along. The sea creature guided him to a floating plank and left him there. After a joyous leap into the air, the creature dived below and vanished.

"As the storm subsided and a blazing sun emerged, Jacques was able to get his bearings. At first all he could see was water, of a transparent turquoise blue unlike any he'd known before. And the remains of the shattered ship, in bits and pieces. Bobbing on the water were hundreds of bottles of wine that had been a large part of the ship's cargo. There was no sign of any other human being, alive or dead.

" 'Marie!' he called out. There was no reply, and he cried out again and again. No human sound responded to his call, and he felt the pain of his loss like a knife through the heart. Why had the sea creature saved his life if he were to live it without the one thing that made it worthwhile?

"And then, just as he had begun to give up hope, he spied something still and white floating a distance away. He paddled closer and saw that it was Marie, unconscious, adrift on a large wooden cargo box, her arms wrapped around a sodden Belle. The dog woofed a melancholy greeting. Jacques reached over and touched Marie's wrist, which was dangling over the side, fearing that he would find her dead and cold. At that moment she opened her eyes and saw Jacques and she smiled weakly.

"They were nearing some sort of land. Jacques paddled and pushed the box carrying Marie and Belle, and with the help of a generous tide, they drifted to shore, washing up on a pristine beach of pink coral sand that had never been touched by humans.

"And so they found themselves on the small, bountiful island, with freshwater streams and fish swimming in the lagoon, so tame that they could reach out and catch them in their hands. They discovered coconuts, crushing the shells on sharp rocks and releasing the milk and sweet insides, and several kinds of lovely fruit, sapodilla and soursop and lime and mango. Of course there were also some of the largest bugs on earth, and a wide assortment of lizards.

"Only a few days after they washed up, Belle retreated to a shady grove and had her puppies. Two were wriggly and healthy, surprisingly black, and less shaggy than their mother. The last, a white female the image of Belle, was stillborn. Marie buried the dead puppy in the woods. She named the island Belle Ile.

"And so," Randall said with a yawn, "that is how the first settlers and the dogs came to Elation Island."

"Wait a minute," said Art. "What the hell happened to them?"

"Oh, that's the sad part."

"*That's* the sad part? The whole thing isn't exactly a laugh riot."

"Well, all right." Randall glanced at his watch and saw that it was five in the morning. "But I'll give the abridged version. I'd like to get *some* sleep before we dock."

He resumed. "At first, Jacques and Marie were blissfully happy. They wore loincloths made out of big leaves. Jacques used the bamboo trees and palm leaves to build them a shelter, and they discovered that the oils from lime rinds and pressed coconuts would sustain the fire they started by striking rocks together to make a spark.

"But Jacques became restless. As he used to do in Brittany, he took to standing at the shoreline staring out at the sea. He knew that there were other islands and a whole continent to explore and he began building a raft, lashing together logs with twine he'd woven from vines. He rigged it with a sail and one day set out alone, assuring Marie he would return in a few short weeks.

"He fully intended to come back, for he still loved Marie above all else. In a few days he came to another island that much resembled Belle Ile, but there was no sign of life. He sailed on. The islands were closer together now, some no bigger than his bedroom in his family's château, some much larger, but not one of them had a sign of a human being. He camped out on the beaches, pushing off at dawn to continue on his journey, until he decided that his search was futile and it was time to go back.

"But along the way he became disoriented and lost. He could not remember the way. As night fell once again and the moon rose, he cried out 'Marie! Marie!' as if she might hear him and guide him. He drifted for days, running out of his supply of fresh water and unable to find any more on the small desolate islands. Eventually the wind took him to New Providence, a lively port town dominated by a community of pirates led by Calico Jack Rackham and his two tough broads, Anne Bonny and Mary Read. It was Anne who found Jacques washed up on the beach.

"She thought him attractive and nursed him back to health. He told her about Marie and Belle Ile, and she promised that one day they would set out to search for the lost island. The pirates were amused by this foolish Frenchman they inevitably nicknamed Frenchie, and invited him to sail with them. He became enamored of the pirate life, the quick thrills and conquests, brazenly ambushing merchant ships from England and Spain, countries he detested.

"After several months he bought a small fishing boat and set out on his search for Belle Ile. He sailed west and south, but he found only the string of empty islands. He began to wonder if he had dreamed it all.

"During the nearly eight months Jacques was gone, much had happened. Marie discovered she was pregnant just after he left. Every day she anxiously awaited his return, only to be disappointed. Belle and her offspring tried to cheer her, but Marie's loneliness and fear kept her awake at night. Every noise frightened her. Her health declined and she went into premature labor, dying in childbirth just as her mother had. The baby, like Belle's puppy, was stillborn.

"Only Belle was there to mourn Marie. Night after night her heartbreaking howls rent the air.

"Jacques returned to New Providence and rejoined the pirate ship. He became a confidant of the notorious Blackbeard, a physical giant who had some fourteen wives. Once, in the climax of a drunken spree, Blackbeard dared his companions, including Frenchie, to enter the hold of a ship where he'd set out trays of burning sulfur. Closing the hatches, he shouted, 'We have made our own hell! Let us now see who is closest kin to the devil by staying longest in it!'

"One by one, his cronies emerged, choking. Frenchie was one of the last out on deck but even he could not compete with Blackbeard, the last to emerge, laughing at all of them.

"It was not long after that incident that the island's governor launched an official campaign to get the pirates out of New Providence. He rounded up a lot of them and threw them in jail. He offered some amnesty, if they'd leave the area and never come back, but he had to make an example of the worst of the lot. In 1717, he hanged them, including Calico Jack, Anne Bonny, Mary Read—and Frenchie.

"Belle Ile languished for over half a century. The dog Belle's offspring bred and inbred and became more wild with each new generation. Ships that sailed close to the island heard the dogs' howls at night and saw them pacing the beaches by day. The British defeated the French in a series of wars and took possession of most of the West Indies. New Providence became Nassau. Belle Ile, for a while referred to in whispers by superstitious French sailors as 'Les Chiens Sauvages' became known by British sailors as 'Elation.' When the American Revolution broke out, loyalists to the King fled to some of the islands, establishing a small colony on Elation Island. They brought slaves with them, who were eventually freed. Later, escaped slaves from the States came, too."

"What about the dogs?" Art pressed.

"Well, when the founding families came, they shot most of the dogs, but a few managed to hide in the hills, forming a small pack that continued to breed and remains wild to this day. Of course, the tourists never see them. Except . . ."

Randall paused, a small smile teasing the corners of his mouth.

"Except what?"

"The legends say that some of the dogs are actually the lost souls of those who have done evil and are destined to wander the hills of Les Chiens forever. They also say that the dogs' howls are Jacques returned to search for his lost Marie."

Randall laughed, breaking the tension he'd created. The others joined him.

"I don't know, Ran," said Jinx. "I liked it better the last time you told it."

Randall got up from his chair. "That's show biz, kiddies. Sweet dreams."

Art continued to sit there, his fingers gripping the arms of the chair.

"I'm not so crazy about dogs," he said in a half-joking tone as Jinx took him by the hand and pulled him to his feet.

"Oh, that's just Randall's crazy idea of a good story," she replied offhandedly as she led him inside through the labyrinth of the yacht's interior and, ultimately, to her bed.

19

"Oh, no, look who's here," said Jinx, pointing to a huge bullet shaped yacht a few hundred feet from where *Charlotte's Web* had anchored. "And in *our* spot."

"The Richardsons." Randall sighed. His hands were clasped around a gin and tonic.

Art looked toward the yacht they were pointing at. It had a bright smiley face under its name: *Pattycakes*, Fort Lauderdale, Florida.

"*Très nouveau*," Randall explained. "A fortune in Twinkie knockoffs."

"God, they'll want to join us, won't they?"

"Let's put out the word we have the plague on board. Or that we're all diabetics."

"But don't you think Art ought to experience Kitty Richardson? 'Why, honey, isn't that *sweet?* Aren't you *precious?*'" she mimicked in an exaggerated southern drawl. "You don't have a blood-sugar problem, do you?"

Art shook his head, trying to rid himself of the nagging fuzziness from not enough sleep and the pressure of being constantly "on."

Elation Island bore no resemblance to the desolate and fearful image Randall had conjured in Art's mind with his story. Instead, Art saw a picturesque pier leading to a small village on the bay side of the island. Art could see the silhouettes of small buildings and the white spire of a church. The land rose in gentle hills away from the water, the vegetation growing denser and greener at the highest point of land. The dock was a long wooden structure set on concrete pylons. There were no boat slips large enough to accommodate yachts the size of *Charlotte's Web* or *Pattycakes*, which dwarfed the many sailboats that dotted the harbor, bobbing at their anchors.

Art followed behind Jinx and Randall, climbing down a stepladder to board a small motored dinghy that drew alongside. Charlotte and Bittles had gone ashore earlier with their friends. Leila and Yves trailed along sleepily. Jinx clutched a mug of coffee and yawned at intervals.

The boat operator was a cheerful black man with a shiny forehead and ropy muscles under his thin shirt and shorts. His feet were bare, thick with calluses. The air smelled of fish and the seaweed that lined the shore like clumps of old hair. As they disembarked, Art saw that a fishing boat was docked at the end of the pier.

Black men, bare torsos gleaming in the sunlight, sorted the slippery catch. Blood and seawater leaked in a spreading pool over the slats of the dock, the blood dripping back into the water, muddying the blue. Art felt his stomach lurch but he could not look away.

"Art, come on," said Jinx, tugging his arm.

He stepped carefully over the row of fish laid out on the planks, their dead eyes staring up at him. The fishermen worked quickly, scraping scales, yanking entrails, and, using machetes, chopped the large grouper into small portions. They wrapped them in newspaper and handed the portions to waiting customers. Black women, heads wrapped in colorful turbans or balancing woven baskets, haggled urgently with the fishermen in singsong accents.

"There's Gray!" said Jinx. A passenger van marked "Elation Island Surf Club" was parked at the entrance to the pier. A sun-weathered white man with thick silver hair climbed out. "Gray, this is Art Glenn, the piano player I told you about. Art, Graham Henderson, he owns the Surf Club."

"Nice to meet you," Art said, putting out his hand and wondering if Gray was actually looking at him. His eyes were hidden behind wraparound black mirrored sunglasses.

"G'day," said Gray. He had the aging, even features of a 1940's movie idol and a vowel-swallowing Australian accent.

Yves and Leila climbed into the back of the

van. Randall sat up front with Gray, Art and
Jinx took the middle row. The van rattled over
the rough wooden slats of the dock and Art felt
his teeth knocking together. The briny smell,
from fish Gray had just purchased, permeated
the air, but no one else seemed bothered. Art
slumped down in the seat, his eyes gritty and
aching behind dark glasses, his nausea rising to
the point where he was afraid he might have to
ask them to stop the van for a quick upchuck
on the side of the road. He swallowed and
clenched his jaw.

They drove onto paved road and the ride improved. The van bounced along the main thor-
oughfare of Johnstown, the island's village.
Small stores lined both sides of the street: a
Piggly Wiggly grocery store, a tiny pharmacy, a
liquor store. They passed the post office, the
Bank of Canada, the Royal Bank of England,
and a pocket-sized Barclay's, American Ex-
press, several taverns, more banks, a bar-disco,
two seafood restaurants, and a Presbyterian
church.

After leaving the town, they headed up an in-
cline, the harbor receding behind them. The ter-
rain roughened in the hills, the neat white
houses giving way to tumbledown shacks and
strung-up laundry, goats tethered in dirt yards.
The van bumped over fallen branches.

"We had a hell of a storm last week," Gray
explained, pointing at the downed trees. "Lost
electricity for two days."

Over the hill the vegetation thickened, the air intoxicating from the heady aromas of flowers and lime trees. Art longed to light up a cigarette but felt it would be somehow sacrilegious. The road opened onto a wide expanse of landscaped grass. They turned and drove through a gate that said "Elation Island Surf Club, Graham Henderson, III, proprietor" and continued along the entranceway, lined on both sides with stately palm trees, trunks perfectly straight and smooth like granite. At the end of the drive, on a hill crest, was a large white Federal-style house facing the ocean. Its broad lawn sloped down to cottages nestled along the dunes. Art could see a croquet course, Ping-Pong tables, tennis courts, and a large swimming pool, looking superfluous in full view of the ocean, surrounded by coral and white deck chairs.

I have come to paradise, Art told himself. I have died and gone to heaven.

Suddenly they were all bustling about. He would have been perfectly happy sleeping the day away in the van, but it seemed that activities had been planned. Black servants came to take their bags.

He carried his own bag before a servant could take it from him. For a moment he could not remember what he had brought with him. In his haste he could have taken anything. His bloodied jacket. But no, he had thrown that away. He followed Jinx, clutching the bag to his chest, as if it might protect him. She left him in a private bungalow, telling him something about being easy to find, since she'd be right next door.

He closed the door and locked it, collapsed on the bed, and fell asleep.

"Art?"

"Yes?" He answered from the depths of sleep, rising level by level into consciousness.

"Art," The tapping on the door came again. "We're going down to the beach. Do you want to come?"

His whole body ached, his mouth tasted foul. "I'll be right there," he muttered.

"Can I come in? I have something for you."

"Uh. Yeah. Okay. Hold on a sec."

He went into the bathroom, rinsed his mouth and peed, came out, and lit a cigarette. He opened the door to find Jinx standing outside in her bikini. The light seared his eyes and he put up his hand to shade them.

"Let's go," he said, putting on his dark glasses.

"Don't you want to change into a swimsuit?" She frowned at the rumpled clothes he'd slept in.

"Well, the funny thing is, I forgot to bring one."

"Oh. Well, Randall probably has an extra, you're about the same size." She put a small silverfoil packet on the table next to the bed.

"Here. A welcome-to-Elation present. I'll go get you a suit."

"Thanks, uh, Jinx."

She paused to smile at him and went back out.

In the packet was a tiny heap of white powder.

He felt hypnotized by the water, undulating toward the shore, and lulled by the sounds of glasses clinking, voices murmuring, the velvet caress of a breeze on his bare white city skin. He reached his hand out and touched the silky coral sand, letting it run through his fingertips.

Jinx rubbed sunscreen all over him, down his back to the top of his buttocks, barely concealed in the tight black spandex suit Randall had loaned him. She did his legs, even between his thighs, as he lay back and just let it happen. When he opened his eyes, Leila was leaning over him, too, her long black hair trailing on his chest. She wore no top and her breasts were small and rounded, with pointy brown nipples. A fierce sexual arousal came over him. He wanted her—both of them—right then and there. He could climb between Leila's tanned legs and live there forever; it reminded him of the first time he had gone down on a woman, he was seventeen and she was older, a coup in itself, and she'd guided his head down and down, while he was amazed, simply astounded that *this was allowed*.

But Leila was only leaning over to take the bottle of suntan lotion from Jinx.

The conversation drifted in and out of his consciousness, like a distant radio station at night.

". . . Galanos's new line, but there was one pale yellow silk . . ."

". . . party in Maroc in April, we must . . ."

". . . produced that film with what'shis name, Sean—"

"Penn—"

". . . so he went back to collecting Fabergé eggs . . ."

"No, I mean Penn and Teller . . ."

Leila rose and sauntered toward the water, diving in and emerging sleek like a seal. He imagined how she would taste, wet and salty. He would catch her and dive under, seize her wriggling legs as she struggled, he would hold his breath till the edge of asphyxiation, then rise, powerful and streaming, wrap her legs around his waist, her bikini bottom floating away like a leaf, her nipples hard against his chest. He would slide into her like butter; the water moving for them, they would follow the rhythm of the waves.

Art rolled over onto his stomach, almost sick with desire. Leila was already back from her swim, her body glistening.

"C'est beau," she said, leaning to one side and jumping in place to shake water from her ears.

He closed his eyes again, willing his body to calm.

Jinx handed around a bag of fruit.

"I'm not hungry," Art said, his throat tight.

"Come on, try it, it's delicious." Jinx was one of those people who thought no was a delayed form of yes. "It's a soursop. You slice it in half, scoop out the inside. Shit, we need a better knife."

"Here," Randall took one from his bag. "L. L. Bean catalog."

He cut the fuzzy brown ball and passed it to Art, who declined once again.

"Did you go to Margo's big bash?" Randall asked Jinx.

Art's head came up fast. Margo? But of course they couldn't be talking about *his* Margo. Hearing the name spoken aloud alarmed him, and for a moment the nausea he'd felt in the van lurched through him again. He looked out at the ocean and saw, walking along the shore, a slim blond woman in a man's white shirt. Her skin was as pale as the sand and Art had a memory, as vivid as the turqoise water, of Margo walking across her kitchen, wearing his white T-shirt that hung just to her bare hips. She opened the refrigerator door and took out a bright red jar. Blood, it was filled with blood. No, that was the dream, the dream of body parts! Margo was asking him something, did he want tomato or orange juice.

He sat up, breathing fast, her name rushing

to his lips, but he stopped himself before the sound came out because the woman by the water paused and turned and, of course, she was a stranger. They were all strangers. The dream, the memory receded, but it left an imprint, like the lingering aura of a flashbulb behind his eyes.

The others were still chattering on. What were they all *talking* about? He felt as if he were in a foreign country, everyone speaking a different language, and he understood only a word here and there. He was becoming invisible. That was why they weren't speaking to him. Well, he could think of a few things to get their attention, a few little conversation stoppers. Like: By the way, I killed someone, her blood ran all over the floor.

"Do you want Perrier?" Jinx was staring at him.

"What?" Had she read his mind? Could they all? Maybe that was why they didn't need to talk to him. They already knew his thoughts. They knew everything.

Jinx repeated her question.

"No, nothing," he said, his voice catching. "A cold beer, maybe."

She passed one over to him.

". . . everyone was there," Randall was saying. "Except you, dear Jinxie, you were the only smart one."

"I had the flu."

"Well, we weren't all so lucky. We were there

five minutes when we saw we were in Deb Hell."
He lowered his voice to a pompous announcer's
pitch. "They thought they were going to a party
but they ended up in *The Night of the Living
Deb!* Depressing, capital *D*. After we left—you
know Clay Weller, from Virginia?— anyway, I
was with his bunch, he knows Margo's brother
from school. We all went down to the World but
it was too late to salvage the night and that's
when I had this incredible revelation!"

Randall paused dramatically. When no one
said anything, he added, "Well, don't you want
to know what it was?"

"Yes," said Jinx, stretching and lying back
down on the blanket.

"Well, I realized that depression and despair
are the only perfect states. Despair is total,
complete, a fait accompli. Whereas happiness
is terribly *flawed*. There's always that little niggling
fear that it will go away soon or—"

Jinx interrupted. "Speaking of nigglings,
could you hail the waiter and get me another
drink?"

"As I was saying, depression is really the perfect
state of being because any change can only
be an improvement! That's how I felt at the
party and then later I went to an all-night coffee
shop where the illegal aliens were putting ammonia
on the floor and stacking the chairs on
the tables. I said to myself: This is total misery.
I have now known perfection. And I threw up
and went home."

"Is anyone else hungry?" Jinx asked. "I know I am."

They sat drinking and eating hors d'oeuvres on the terrace overlooking the ocean. The sun was already beginning to dip low on the horizon. Art held a planter's punch with a little umbrella and fruit sticking out over the rim of a mammoth glass that was stabbing him in the mouth. Finally, he stripped the drink of its decorations and drank it down, tasting salt, rum, and fruit, mixed with cocaine. The steel-drum band finished their set and was replaced by a small pop combo. The lead singer was a young woman with an old-fashioned perky sound that piqued his memory, and all at once he was a small boy sitting at the front table watching his mother, Lila Noone, frozen in time.

He went into the hotel lounge, the decor an eccentric mix of floral prints, and tipped up the cover of the baby grand piano. He placed his hands on the keys, imagining the sound before touching with enough force to create it, like running his fingertips over a woman's skin in the first tantalizing exploration. He pressed down, sounding a pure chord, then shifted for another.

He could see himself, from a distance, he was a camera looking down at the scene, the floral room, the piano, the piano player who had all the time in the world, all the talent in the world.

It was a good piano, mellow, easy action, with

enough resistance to make it feel alive under his hands. He didn't know what to play, so he let the hands decide.

They chose to play "Bewitched."

People were flocking around, as he knew they would, as they always did. He finished that song and started taking requests. He knew everything, and of course they were impressed, an older crowd who wanted to hear Gershwin and Porter and Arlen, and he obliged, the perfect music slave.

He played until dark, the last hint of sun drowning on the horizon. The insects came out and added their concerto, and for a moment, when he stopped playing, when just for a second the conversational roar of the party dipped to an uncharacteristic hush, Art thought he could hear, in the far distance, the howl of an animal.

20

When she moved her head, she felt the world lurch.

There was a sticky, sickening taste in her mouth that she slowly identified as her own blood. For a long time she had no idea who she was or where, or why there was so much blood and such a splintering universe in her head.

She opened her eyes and saw a desert and hills, boulders and small animals, and gradually came to understand that she was looking at a floor, at the peeling, raised fragments of ruined linoleum, and at the lives of busy, indifferent roaches.

Surely someone would come and help her. But no one did and she drifted in and out of consciousness, her sleep a false one filled with demons.

She didn't know how long she had lain there when some basic instinct finally moved her to get up. Seizing hold of a table leg to help her stand, weak and hurting, she staggered into the bathroom. It was a dark and suffocating red, as if the walls too had bled, and she stood for a moment, terribly confused, until she figured out that it was only the wallpaper.

There was an ugly stranger in the mirror. Her hair was matted with dried blood and the side of her face was a mass of colors. She threw up into the sink.

It came back to her how he had just left her there to die, and at first she couldn't believe it, because he had seemed so nice.

Maybe she *had* died. What evidence did she have that this life was actually hers? It would have been easy for someone to steal her brain and put it in another body.

She wrapped her head in a soiled towel which reddened from the still-seeping blood, and struggled down the stairs. On the street, people stared or looked away. She wandered with a vague sense of where she was going, reeling like a drunk. She grabbed hold of parked cars to steady herself and kept going, block after agonizing block, knowing the hospital was up there someplace and she had to get to it. After a while a man helped her, asked her what was wrong, took her by the arm and supported her the last few blocks to the emergency room at Bellevue.

They cleaned her up and stitched her and took an X ray of her head. She waited a very long time, lying on a rolling cot in a white room, staring up at the ceiling. They wanted to know her name but she was smart enough not to tell them. They'd only use it against her. The room was cold and she wondered if she was in the morgue, except that she could hear someone moaning behind a curtain a few feet away. She stared up at the cracked ceiling that looked like spider webs, and she thought about when she was a skinny little kid and followed a bunch of boys in her neighborhood to a rubbishy part of Canarsie by the landfills. They liked to go exploring in the dumps.

One of the boys yelled out and called the others around. Susan trailed along behind them, wanting to see what they saw, to feel the raw, wild power of the boys, to belong with them. They were clustered around a spider making its way across the ground. The spider was hugely swollen, its black hairy legs sticking out from its round body. One of the boys picked up a stick and nudged at it but the spider continued on its way. The boys pursued it, each daring the other to pick it up or kill it.

"No," someone shouted, "get Susan." And then she was up in the air over their shoulders, wriggling like a fish, but there were too many of them and they were too strong. They took her hand and pushed it down onto the body of the spider, bursting it beneath the pressure of her flesh like a ripe fruit.

Hundreds of tiny spiders exploded from the crushed body, madly dashing this way and that.

Susan screamed and screamed until the sound turned into an inhuman noise, a hoarse honking. The boys got scared and they scattered, running, their savage shrieks echoing behind them, until the only sound was coming from her. When she finally stopped screaming, sick with exhaustion, she thought she had lost her sight. The sky was a blinding white, the world a white cold and she felt she had been turned inside out, and all within her was made of ice.

She lay in the cold white room for a long time, occasionally reaching up to feel the fresh bandage keeping her brains inside her head for now. The hospital people came in and told her there were no beds, like what the fuck was she lying on? They didn't seem to like that she had no Blue Cross insurance. They asked her if she could get up now and she had the feeling it was an order, so she rolled herself off the cot and stood, holding on to the edge for balance. Before she'd even gotten out of the room they were ripping the paper covering off the cot and she knew they were planning to keep it as evidence against her. When they saw that she could stand they seemed pleased and sent her into another room to see a social worker.

As if she needed their help. She didn't even want their hands touching her and she knew for certain, as she sat in the waiting area, that at least five people were trying to poison her with their laser stares.

And then the social worker was that blond she

had seen with *him* at Jack's. Obviously, this was a warning, an omen. She'd have to be very careful about what she revealed.

After she left the hospital, she went back to Gloria's.

In her fucked-up state she'd left the door unlocked, the last thing she needed was to look around for a key, but when she got back she couldn't get in. Her head hurt a lot and all she wanted was to lie down. She thought maybe she was in the wrong building but the hall looked just the same. She heard voices inside and she knocked hard. Gloria opened the door.

Susan stepped back in surprise. Gloria was supposed to be away at least another week.

"So there you are," Gloria was saying, her eyes narrow with anger, "I come back and my fucking door is wide open, I mean, here I'm doing you a favor letting you stay and I find the place trashed." There was a man standing behind Gloria. He had dark curly hair pulled back into a ponytail. Susan could see Gloria's duffle bag on the table.

Susan stood on the threshold, certain she was going to faint.

"Guy tried to kill me," she muttered.

"And why the hell is there blood all over the kitchen? I thought I'd find a dead body but *no*, just a big disgusting mess." Gloria was pacing around, pointing at this and that. The guy was browsing through the refrigerator. "I told you, Susan, when I let you stay, that you had to take care of the place. So why don't you just go, okay? I swear, you try to do nice for some people and look at what you get."

Susan pulled the wool blanket tight around her body and up over head to keep out the cold as she walked along, up Broadway, past Lincoln Center, where well-dressed people were getting out of taxis and limousines and hurrying into the grand theaters. She was an Eskimo in her disguise, no one could see more than her eyes, which lasered out like knives at the people. Before they could get her. The bandages on her head were no longer white. They hung off at an angle, exposing black stitches on bare chicken flesh, where they'd shaved her. It made her sick to look at it but she'd lost her mirror anyway.

She was tired and it was already well past dark but that didn't matter, she could sleep in the bus terminal all day tomorrow. The only thing she had to worry about was being hassled by lunatics, but she'd found that a combination of The Look and a deep growl sometimes scared them off. And when she had her weapon she would be safe all the time.

At 72nd Street, she saw the ghost of the old Susan standing on the corner handing out Clancy fliers. At least it had been warm then. Now it was all ruined. Clancy's was closed, with notices from the government pasted over the front door. Maybe they had her name, too.

She stopped when she got to Jack's and

looked in through the window. His picture was still there. The Piano Stylings of Art Glenn. But he had not yet returned. The little guy was there instead, the one who sang songs she never heard before.

Susan kept walking, although she stopped sometimes if people on the street crowded her. She gave them The Look, just in case. If they only knew that inside her were thousands of tiny poison spiders, ready to burst out. To keep them from spilling out of her mouth or her ears or any of her orifices, she carefully counted everything, although some numbers were dangerous colors. She hurried past Seventy-ninth Street, a number that glowed dark evil green. A pay phone was ringing at the corner and she picked it up, sure there would be a message for her, but there was no voice on the other end. The number written on the phone was three even, four odd: blue, red, red; green, yellow, orange, green. She dropped it like a live coal. They weren't going to fool her that easily.

She paused at 86th Street, begged some change and took the subway all the way up to 145th. She wasn't sure of the address anymore but knew she'd recognize the building by its graffiti, a network of tiny swastikas that looked like a spider's web until you got close and saw what it was. Susan didn't understand why people got so uptight about swastikas. What she didn't like about the wall was the web.

The outside door to the building was missing,

the inner one hanging on half a hinge. The stair-well smelled of urine and stale cooking fat. She went up to the third floor and knocked. There was no answer. She knocked again, louder. She could hear a radio playing salsa in another apartment and a baby crying up on the next floor.

She sat down on the stairs to wait and fell asleep, leaning her bandaged head against the broken bannister.

It seemed only a few minutes later that a noise woke her, but her neck was so stiff she knew she must have been sitting there a much longer time.

Someone was coming up the stairs. Two men. She could hear their voices. For a second she was afraid it was Boyd, until she remembered with relief that he was at Rikers.

No, it was Joey, and when he saw Susan, his eyes went all wide, like she'd come back from the dead or something. Joey was small and stringy, his pale skin pocked with sores from sticking needles into himself and living on po-tato chips and Ring Dings and Cokes. He was with another man, a short, stocky black man who was talking fast in a low complaining voice.

"I need to sleep a coupla hours," she said, coming right to the point.

"Jesus Christ, you look like fuckin' Friday the 13th. Gimme a break, man, I got no room, and I got customers. They don't wanna look at no horror flick."

"Just a coupla hours. I've got some bread."

"For Chrissake."

She gave him The Look.

"What the fuck's the matter with you?"

"I could answer the phone."

"What fucking phone?"

"Just gimme a coupla hours."

"For shit's sake."

"Hey, dude," said the other man, "I don't have all fuckin' night."

Joey opened the door with his key and the three of them went inside. There were two rooms. In the first, there were some stained mattresses on the floor, about a dozen old take-out bags, empty Styrofoam and paper coffee cups, pieces of newspapers, tiny crack vials. The sink was broken, halfway out of the wall, the pipes showing, and the refrigerator stank.

She went straight into the second room and saw more mattresses, one with a pillow that had the word Firm written all over it. The apartment hadn't changed since Susan was there a few months before, helping Joey deliver crack to some of his scuzzball clients.

While Joey was hassling with the black guy in the other room, Susan opened the closet door, remembering how Joey, full of drugs and shit, had shown her his little arsenal, as he'd called it.

She pulled out the cardboard box, making as little sound as possible. The arsenal had shrunk considerably. He must have had to sell the big-

ger ones he'd shown her, lifting each one out of
the box like a baby, clicking it and aiming at
the window, then putting it lovingly away.

There were just two guns left. One of them
had a long blunt-looking barrel that would be
hard to carry around and conceal. The other
was smaller, more compact, with a nice wooden
handle. She picked it up gingerly. On the side it
said, Smith & Wesson .38 SPL. She had no idea
if it was even loaded and didn't want to take
the time to look. Besides, it would be good
enough to scare off the lunatics, so she slipped
it beneath the blanket that was wrapped around
her, closed the drawer and walked out of the
room.

Joey and the other guy were measuring some
white powder into a piece of tinfoil.

"Needs more talc," the black guy was saying.

"You wanna get me fuckin' killed, man?"

"I gotta go to the store for some stuff," Susan
said, but neither of the men bothered to look
up.

21

Barbecue smoke wafted over the tables. The calypso band was playing again—a rousing, hollow clinking "Lemon Tree" on steel drums. The sun hovered at the edge of the horizon. Graham Henderson moved among the tables, collecting bets from the guests on how long it would take the sun to sink behind the horizon, bottom edge to top edge. Fifteen minutes? Eight minutes? One? Art thought hard before placing his bet: six and a half minutes. He felt cheated when the great orange globe disappeared in less than three.

Luminously drunk, he raised his voice in song with the band, beating time on the table with his swizzle stick. He was probably the best drunk at the whole hotel.

A waft of perfume preceded the woman as she leaned over him and said in a sultry tone, "You *know* you're just fabulous. You *know* that, don't you?"

Without waiting for a reply—which he didn't have—she went right on. "A natural, isn't that what they call someone like you? I bet you never took a lesson in your life, you were just *born* playing, am I right?" She had metallic silver-blond hair shellacked off her face into a tight knot. Black liner rimmed her eyes. "I'm Taffy Richardson." She held out her hand. When he took it, he felt something pressing against his palm. "Please, please, please play my all-time favorite, 'Song Sung Blue.' I think you sound just like Neil Diamond. I guess you never wanted to be a big star like him, though, right? Preferred the quieter side of things?" She petted his hand, which was clutching the bill she'd slipped him. When she walked away, he saw that it was a hundred.

"So how do you like our island?" It was Graham Henderson, the Aussie, standing nearby.

"I think I've died and gone to heaven."

Gray laughed. "It's a good life. Come on, I'll show you around. I used to be in the business, too, y'know."

Art stood up with some difficulty, taking his drink with him. He dutifully followed the trim, fit Gray, who was built like a marine even though he must be sixty at least. They entered the hotel lobby and Gray slid the glass doors shut behind them, muffling the sounds of music and ocean.

The sudden quiet was like a blanket smothering him. What did this guy want? Was he gay or something?

Gray showed Art into his private office, a small, crowded room. The walls were filled with framed photos as well as some strange objects. Art's attention was caught by a large knife with a fierce curving blade. It hung below a worn old bush hat, pinned up on one side and decorated with military medals.

"Nasty lookin' job, eh?" said Gray, tapping the knife. "Gurkha knife, y'know. They call it a kukri. Picked it up when I was fightin' Japs in Burma 'longside a Gurkha unit. Those fuckers were the toughest bastards you'd ever see. Glad they were on our side. Saw one of them kill a Jap with his bare hands and slice his head right off his body."

"With his hands?"

"No." Gray looked at Art sharply. "With his knife."

"I was . . . uh . . . kidding."

"Ah. Of course." Gray pointed to a photo near his desk. "There's yours truly with MacArthur. Came through right after I was made lieutenant." He pronounced it *leftenant*.

"Must have been an exciting time," Art said, feeling uneasy as he always did around military men.

"Best of our lives. Those that stayed alive. I still got two bullets in my chest, too dangerous to have them taken out. Sets off the metal detectors whenever I go through airport security."

Gray led Art to the other side of the room. "Here's the stuff I really wanted to show you. I came to the States after the War, that's where the business was. People hardly know I'm an Aussie anymore, I been around Americans s'long."

Art glanced at his host, to see if he was joking. He wasn't.

There were more framed photos but these were publicity shots of a young, sleek Gray, with thick wavy blond hair, standing and evidently crooning behind a fat radio microphone. More pictures showed him beside Kate Smith; in another, he was paired with Bing Crosby, who was looking in the opposite direction, as if someone had just called his name. Several photos were of big bands with Gray as the singer. An old program advertised Manny Carter and His Harmony Orchestra Featuring the Song Stylings of Graham Henderson.

"So, uh, did you, uh, give up or something?" Art asked.

"Yeah. The business stinks. Then. Now. It's all the same. Everyone's out for blood. Sure, I could have been a big star." He snapped his fingers. "But then what?"

Gray pointed to more photos on the opposite wall. "That's the family. My wife, she was a contract player at MGM, we met when I went out there on a tour and got on a picture."

"What picture?"

"Nothin' you'd remember. They kept her in B pix so she said forget it and came down here with me when I bought the property. Land was cheap then, nobody wanted it. I always wanted to run my own place. You have to hang on to your dignity or they'll strip it away from you. Hey, don't listen to me, you're young, you got it all ahead of you. If this were the '40's you could make it into films, playing piano in all those nightclub scenes. Like that guy . . . whatshisname, he's on the videos the kids watch, white guy, sounds like he's black—"

"Harry Connick Jr.?"

"Yeah, that's the one. Somebody's promoting that career, huh?"

Not wanting to ponder the successes of rival club pianists, Art looked up the wall again. "Isn't that—?"

"Right. Ronald Reagan. Sure, we knew them, my wife worked with Nancy—Davis, then. Cute girl, Nancy, not much talent. Great legs."

"Well," said Art, ready to leave. Gray was staring at the walls, his face older.

"Yeah. It was a kick, back then. A bloody great life."

"Well, I guess I'd better go sing for my supper. . . ."

"No hurry." Gray sat down behind his desk and pulled out some files. He began to leaf through a packet of yellowing photographs and clippings. Art stood a few feet away, unsure what he was supposed to do next. But Gray seemed to have forgotten him and didn't notice when he slipped out.

He took a wrong turn outside Gray's office and wound up exiting through a door that led to a path down to the water. The sky had darkened quickly, the beach shrouded in a fine shadowy mist. With the music at his back, he stumbled onto the sand, still warm like flesh beneath his bare feet. It surprised him because he couldn't remember taking off his shoes.

"For those in peril on the sea!" he sang, remembering only the tag line of the old marine hymn. The waves were coming in harder, stamping on the shore. "For those in peril on the sea . . ."

He could walk straight in, like Norman Maine, and sleep, and sleep.

"Here you are! I feel like I'm always looking for you. They want you, Artie, they want you to play." Jinx grabbed his hand and led him back inside. "Here he is! Here's our piano player!"

He could see the calypso band standing to one side of the room, smoking cigarettes, looking at him, the square white guy.

He played a twelve-bar blues, slow and funky, but when he looked over to see their reaction, the calypso musicians were nowhere in sight. And anyway, he'd run out of clever blues riffs.

He played "Bewitched, Bothered and Bewildered," realizing after he started that he played it earlier, so he switched keys, into "Send in the

Clowns," but that came out wrong, too. He couldn't seem to find the right chords, so he meandered around until he landed on "Someone to Watch Over Me" but that turned into "Bewitched" again.

Maybe the guests thought he was creating some kind of brilliant medley, but his hands shook and his pulse was going haywire. He closed his eyes, tried again. This time, his traitorous hands started playing "Don't Cry Out Loud."

He stopped and stared down at them, the wretched little animals. He took a deep breath and dug into the three opening notes of "Summertime" but "sum-mer-time" turned into "don't-cry-out."

Nearly crying with frustration, he pounded his hands down on the keys. The guests were looking up, distracted by this sudden noise, this interruption in their background ambience.

Jinx was at his side. "What's the matter?" she whispered.

"*Nothing.*"

He played "Bewitched."

"We've *heard* that already."

"I like it."

"Mama wants 'It Had to Be You.' "

Then let *her* play it, he thought but didn't say. He tried to oblige, but the first three notes became "don't cry out." This time he played the rest of the song, hoping to purge it from his system so that the others could come back.

"Well, if you're going to be the temperamental musician about it," Jinx said, stomping away.

Randall came over as Art was playing "Don't Cry Out Loud" for the fourth time in a row. "I believe in artistic freedom," Randall proclaimed drunkenly. "You play whatever you want to play." He laid a heavy hand on Art's shoulder, squeezed slightly. "You having a good time?"

Art nodded stiffly.

"That's good. Because that's all that matters. In life. Having a good time. One minute you're alive, the next minute you're dead. *Poof!*" He laughed. "*Poof! Dead poofter!*" Randall leaned in close to Art's ear. "Lissen, you come over to my suite, I have something'll make you feel better."

Art followed Randall dutifully into the bungalow. Yves was stretched out on the bed, wearing only bikini briefs that barely covered a half-mast erection. There was a vaguely familiar, sweetly chemical smell in the air. Art looked from one man to the other as it dawned on him that they'd misunderstood.

Randall handed Art a glass filled with Scotch and leaned over the night table. The light from the lamp illuminated his face grotesquely, the skin stretched over the bones. He offered an inhaler to Art, who realized that the smell was amyl nitrate.

"No, that's okay," he said. "A little too fucked up right now."

"Straighten you right out."

Yves got up and went into the bathroom. Art could hear him urinating into the bowl and the flush of the toilet. Randall opened his suitcase and took out a black object.

Fear flashed through Art like an electric shock.

Yves came out of the bathroom, a towel around his shoulders, and said something to Randall in French. They both laughed, a private sound.

Art could feel the sting of amyl nitrate in his nostrils, even though he hadn't breathed it in directly.

Randall was holding up a black leather mask, its empty sockets grinning.

"Would you like to play?" he asked Art, innocently, as if he were suggesting a round of pinochle.

"I—no, thanks, that's not my scene."

"Never know till you try it. Look, you're tense, anyone can see that. We'll do whatever you want, no problem. It's all safe, you know. Cellophane, rubbers, the whole plague shebang."

He could hear their laughter as he fled.

He wanted to go back to his bungalow but he couldn't remember which one it was. Maybe if he called someone, made a long-distance call.

He hadn't noticed if there was a phone in his room but there must be one at the main house.

The dark sea beckoned, the tide creeping closer with each wave, whispering for him to come along.

He turned the other way and began to jog along the path that led up the hill from the stately white mansion. The wind had picked up and was shoving him along from behind, as if it knew where it wanted him to go. He continued up, into the woods where the dense brush and palms kept even the glowing white moon from finding him. He slowed, snared by vines, but kept on, his breath coming harsh now, searing his lungs until he could no longer hear anything but his own gasping and the distant *penk-pank* of steel drums.

He still clutched the glass, most of the drink spilled in his run, but he sipped at the dregs, a melting ice cube bumping his front teeth. The clink of the ice was loud. He walked on a little farther and found himself in a clearing. The night sky had filmed over, high gray clouds like fish scales, the moon sliding in and out of sight. He had the sensation of the earth speeding up, preparing to hurl itself out of orbit. From somewhere nearby came the impertinent *baa* of a goat.

Art climbed the hill until he reached its apex and could see the shape of the island below: the lights of Johnstown and the harbor, the glow from Gray Henderson's Surf Club. A goat bleated again and he peered through the dark to find it. He was beginning to breathe easier now, sobering up and feeling slightly foolish. What a schmuck he was. He sank wearily to the cool grass, set down the empty glass, and rested his face in his hands.

A growl startled him. He peered through the shadows but could see nothing. Perhaps it had been a distant rumble of thunder. But no, there was something approaching. A dog. A wraith of a dog was slinking toward him. The terror he'd felt at Randall's story came back and it was as if all of his life had been leading up to this moment.

I'm going to die, I'm going to fucking die.

He saw it like a deep black pit and it was almost a relief, until he saw that at the bottom of the pit hideous things were writhing, reaching up their bloodied tentacles.

He could hear the screech of a car's brakes on some highway, someone screaming in pain, the screams of a woman bursting from her mouth, the terror of her own death, the explosion of her body into mangled bits of flesh and bone and blood.

He saw a woman's body lying on a tenement floor, blood soaking around her, rising, like a tide.

Another low growl, this one from behind.

Art sat absolutely still, frozen in fear. A third sound came from his right, a low whine that went on and on. More dogs approached, forming a circle around him, keeping at a peculiar distance of four or five feet. Some of them simply stared at him; others licked at themselves, at sores or fleas or private parts.

In the background the drone went on, the murmurs and wails and moans of the dying, the dead, in fragments of crushed cars and planes falling from the sky, the staccato hammering of machine guns, all blending into a swelling crescendo that turned into the mingled howls of a hundred feral dogs. Yet the shadowy dogs he could barely make out in a sliver of moonlight were still and silent.

He had done some terrible thing and now he was lost.

"Belle," he whispered.

One of the dogs turned its snout up and bayed at the moon, an eerie sound that was neither animal nor human.

Art felt the hairs on his arms and his neck prickle. Chemicals were running wild in his veins, blood rushing under his skin. He whimpered when the largest dog rose to its feet and snuffled nearer.

He felt around for the empty glass and hurled it wildly, hearing it smash against a rock. There was a flurry among the dogs, a ripple of growls and short barks, as if they were discussing his action and deciding their next move.

The largest dog bared its fangs, which seemed to glow like radium. For a moment all was still. Even the wind rested. Then the dogs, as one, began to edge closer, shrinking the circle. He reached down for a stone, fingers grasping in the dirt, and found weeds, twigs, pebbles, but no stones, no cudgel, no weapon. Moaning, he dug in with both hands, scraping desperately until his fingers came upon a stone, hard and smooth, and he hurled it at the biggest dog.

It missed, careened off a tree and into the brush.

He looked up at the moon and howled his anguish. The ungodly wailing in the air had stopped and now the silence pressed in.

The dogs stopped slinking closer, confused. He howled again, an animal sound that tore his throat. He scrambled up and began running down the other side of the hill, sharp rocks cutting his bare feet. He was certain he could feel the snapping jaws at his heels and he stumbled and fell, rolling and rolling down, twigs cracking against his face; he tumbled down to the bottom of the hill, coming to rest against a broken palm tree.

There were no dogs in sight, not the hint of a dog, and he began to cry, like a baby.

"Good God, I'm sorry, please please just help me."

Suddenly he heard something stirring closer.

"Oh, no more, please." It was rustling the bushes, a snuffling sound, getting nearer. He could not move. He was beaten. Let it come.

It leaned in, warm breath on his face, and licked his cheek.

It was a goat.

He laughed sharply and the animal drew back, gave a bewildered *beehhh*, echoed by the sharp cry of a rooster, like an alarm clock going off too early. The goat trotted away and began to nibble at the grass.

He waited there for a long time until even the moon had fled and there was nothing but black starless night. He wanted to be safe at home but he realized that there was no place he could call home and there never had been. There was no safe place.

He thought of Margo and said aloud: "I love you in all the warm and sunny places in the universe. I love you in all the stars and the planets," and he wondered if, somehow, she could hear him. He closed his eyes and imagined lifting out of his body, soaring over the sea to the mainland, up over Florida and North Carolina and Washington, D.C., and New Jersey, all the way up to New York, where she lay sleeping. He squeezed his eyes shut and visualized her and tried to send an SOS.

It was all so much clearer now, what he would have to do. He could even see himself walking into a police station and telling them the whole thing. After all, he had not deliberately hurt that girl. It was an accident and they would have to believe him because he was not the kind of person who killed. He was Art Glenn and all he wanted to do was play the piano and have people like him.

Margo was another problem altogether, but at least he could try to win her back.

He felt in his pockets. His only still-good credit card was there, although he wouldn't be surprised if they'd canceled that one, too, for back bills. And he had some cash, including Taffy Richardson's hundred-dollar bill. There was really no reason at all to return to the Surf Club. He supposed that Charlotte and her set would never hire him again. So be it. So much for his career in high society. There was always Jack's.

At last, shivering from the chilly dew that had begun to coat the predawn island, he rose stiffly to his feet and began walking down the hill toward the town. As the sun slowly rose, he could see that he was passing through a cemetery, the random headstones bending over, as if they were too tired to stand up straight. Old stones and wooden crosses with names and dates smoothed out by time. He could read a few of them. "Mary Albury 1807–1841." "James Albury 1805–1850." "Johnnie Albury 1837–1840." Lives so brief, so forgotten. He hurried on.

The dirt path widened, passing behind the rows of shanty houses, built haphazardly close together, yard spilling against yard, chickens pecking randomly at the ground, goats tethered, a few stringy cats. He came to a large wooden building that rose out of the mist. A small hand-carved sign was stuck in the dirt:

"Holy Roller Baptist Church Built 1865. Elation Island, B.W.I."

He continued on to the paved road, the houses larger with tidy gardens in front and back and low picket fences bordered by cascading bougainvillea and frangipani. The sun was a faint glow on the horizon, casting its speckled early light on the water. Then he was walking out onto the pier. A few fishing boats were preparing to head out. He sat on a bench and watched the men as they loaded nets and buckets of bait.

Realizing he had no idea how he was going to get off this island, he approached one of the men.

"How do I get to the mainland?"

The black fisherman looked at his friends then stared at Art. It occurred to Art that he was a mess, his clothes rumpled and muddy from his mad flight.

"I have money," he added, instinctively touching his pocket. Now they came to life, nodding and talking among themselves in a thick dialect that sounded like cockney English mixed with French and pidgin. The one Art had spoken to first said something that sounded like "Habey goin' lutra." Art shook his head and the man repeated it until he understood that the man named Abe was taking his boat to Eleuthera Island to visit his family and from there Art could get a flight to the States.

The men stared pointedly at his shabby clothes.

"I fell down," he explained. "I got lost and was chased by the dogs."

They looked at him blankly.

"You know, the wild dogs in the hills. Woof, woof!"

The men grinned, their teeth startlingly white in dark faces. One of them said, "No dogs on 'Lation. No dogs for hundred years."

Another added gleefully, "Dogs in the whiskey!" and they all got a good laugh, repeating "dogs in the whiskey" over and over.

Art offered fifty dollars for his passage and they all seemed pleased. When Abe asked if he had "the grip," at first Art thought they meant he was coming down with the flu, until he realized they were talking about a suitcase. He hesitated, thinking about his overnight case back at the bungalow, then he shook his head and followed the fisherman onto the small boat.

22

When Margo couldn't sleep, she tried listing things in her mind.

Sometimes she counted major league baseball teams; first, the National League with twelve teams, then the American, which inexplicably had fourteen. This bothered her. Why didn't the American League give one to the National and then they'd be even? Or was it because neither wanted to have thirteen?

Ordinarily, thinking along these lines put her right to sleep, but not tonight.

She decided to count lovers. Once, when she was about twenty-seven and beginning to lose track, she made a list, including names, approximate dates of the affair or one-night stand, each man's astrology sign, which seemed interesting at the time, and a rating system for orgasmic success—hers. Theirs was never a problem. The few before Michael—or "B.M.," as she termed it—were a dispiriting bunch. Or she had been a lousy partner, because she rarely came. With Michael, she always came. The dozen or so after him were hit-and-miss, but generally she'd managed to pull victory from the jaws of defeat, so to speak.

In the shadowy dark of her bedroom, with the sounds of late-night traffic on the street below, an occasional fire-engine siren punctuating the night, she counted: one, John, Pisces; two, Eddie, Libra; three, Michael, Capricorn . . .

What she needed was a change of scene. A trip. She would take a leave from her job, sublet the apartment, and travel. Paris. London. The Greek Islands. Sometimes she even missed the theater, wondering if perhaps she'd run away from it too soon, for the wrong reasons. Or was wanting to return to it a way of running away from life? Travel, of course, was running away from everything.

Maybe she'd move out of New York altogether. Everyone else was. Her friends and colleagues were divided into two camps: those who couldn't stand the city anymore and were planning to leave and those who couldn't stand the city anymore but didn't know how to leave.

She turned over in bed and lay on her stomach for a while until her back began to hurt. She touched herself tentatively but that made her even more acutely aware of how lonely she was, how much she missed Art, and so she stopped. The digital clock radio showed that it was twenty-three minutes after midnight. Not all that late, except that she had to get up early and had been trying to fall asleep since eleven.

She got up and switched on the light, blinking as her eyes adjusted.

She hadn't heard from him in almost a week, but she hadn't tried to get in touch with him either, other than calling the club the night of their breakup. Before the thought reached her brain, she was dialing the phone.

"Jack's."

"Hello. Is . . . Art Glenn there?"

"Nope."

"Do you expect him?"

"He's out of town. Who knows when he'll turn up?"

"Thanks." She put down the receiver.

It hadn't occurred to her she might never see him again. Or that she would care so much.

She put on her warm, frayed robe and went into the living room. As she turned on the light, she felt that old instant reflex: fear of seeing a roach darting down the wall. She stood still, watching the walls, the floors, for movement, but there was nothing. The room was chilly and she remembered she'd opened a window earlier in the day, when the sun was warm, and now she went to close it. As she drew the curtain, she paused for a moment, looking out. Someone was standing in the shadows of the scaffolded building across the street, the one that was being renovated, and the person appeared to be looking up at her window.

She drew back, startled. Switching off the light, she peeked out through the curtain from the dark. Yes, there was someone there. The street lamp cast just enough light on the figure for illumination, but Margo could not tell if it was a man or a woman. It wore a dark hood or something shadowing the face, and a shapeless dark coat. The person really did seem to be watching Margo's building and the fourth floor in particular.

Her imagination, fed by a lifetime of television and old movies, considered stakeouts, spies, detectives, hit men, maniacs. Her pragmatic side told her that it was probably a druggie waiting for a dealer. Or a hooker waiting for a john. Or just someone waiting to meet a late-night date.

Margo closed the window all the way. She locked it, too, although no one was likely to scale the wall. Unless her building was being surveilled by that guy who suctioned his way up the World Trade Center.

Still, she was unaccountably nervous and turned on the radio to fill the room with sound. Jazz warmed the spaces and she took a deep breath, let it out, and took another one.

Probably she wouldn't have felt paranoid at all if she hadn't had the same feeling, earlier that day, that she was being followed. It was when she left the clinic. The hour was not late but it was already dark, and as she walked down First Avenue to the crosstown bus on

Twenty-third, she had the creepy sensation someone was behind her. She even paused to look around, but she didn't see anyone suspicious. Of course, in New York, everyone could look suspicious if you were jittery enough. She'd long ago learned to be alert without being actively afraid.

Deciding that she was being ridiculous, she sat down at her cluttered desk and began to go over the patients' files that were stacked precariously, paperwork she'd fallen behind on. Half of her job was filling out forms for an idiotic, numbing bureaucracy.

Opening the top file, she read over the case of Doris, an elderly woman sadly typical of the people Margo saw, both at the hospital clinic and the shelter. Doris had been a schoolteacher in New York City for thirty years, according to her own statement, but was unable to make do on her small pension. She had a grown daughter living in California and a son in Virginia, but they had lost touch with their mother. Margo had tried to contact them several times. She managed to find the son, but he said he had his own problems. He was out of work and his wife had left him. Doris had become ill over the years, physically and mentally. Her apartment was lost to a co-op conversion and she moved in with a sister, until that situation became unbearable and she was asked to leave. The sister helped Doris out financially until she died four years ago and Doris ended up on the streets and in the shelter system. She has periods of acute disorientation, Margo had noted, ulcerated legs and suffers from incontinence. She was asked to leave several shelters because the volunteers hadn't the resources or the training to cope with her. The hospitals couldn't provide a bed for more than a few nights at a time.

And you think you've got troubles, Margo thought.

She wrote a brief evaluation of Doris, recommending that she be hospitalized, with or without her consent, at least until her leg sores healed and she was stabilized on medication.

Margo moved on to the next file, recalling the young woman quite clearly. The patient had come into the emergency room one night last week with a badly bleeding head injury. Margo had taken a colleague's shift at the last minute, welcoming the opportunity to work herself into exhaustion to help put Art out of her mind. The patient was a mess, the wound almost twenty-four hours old, and she'd lost a lot of blood. But the examining doctor ascertained that the wound was superficial, so he stitched her up and referred her to Margo for a psych evaluation.

Margo called the woman into her office, which was nothing more than a cubicle separated from identical cubicles by a faded green plasterboard wall. Inside there was an institutional-gray metal desk and two plastic chairs. The woman sat down uneasily, after looking all around and up at the ceiling. She was sickly looking, her head bandaged and her hair dirty where it showed, and she was wrapped in a hospital blanket they'd given her in the emergency room. She kept rubbing her cheek in a nervous, compulsive gesture. There was something vaguely familiar about the woman, but Margo couldn't quite place her. Perhaps she'd seen her at one of the shelters or on the street. Or perhaps the woman just resembled someone else.

"Are you having headaches?" Margo asked. The woman had refused to give her last name. The admitting nurse had written "Susan Doe" on the file.

"Yeah, my head hurts, what do you think?" She looked at Margo, her gaze rigid and intense, and Margo felt a stirring of anxiety.

"How did you get this injury?"

"Guy knocked me down. Tried to kill me. But he couldn't break through the aura."

"Do you take drugs, Susan? Crack?"

"I don't do that shit."

"You say someone tried to kill you. Do you know who it was?"

"Oh, yeah, I know him. He's famous." The woman gave Margo the weird, unnerving stare again.

"Have you reported this to the police?"

"I don't look very good."

"What do you mean?"

"When they put my picture in the paper. I mean, look at me." She lowered her voice to a confidential whisper. "We can't let it get out. Yet. It's not time. All the media. 'The Oprah Winfrey Show.' My hair has to grow back in. You see, I have power and everyone will want it, but I'm not ready yet. The world will explode if I let them know. That girl that bit me on the street? She nearly gave me AIDS but I lasered her!"

Margo sighed. "Do you want to be tested for AIDS?"

"I have a protective aura."

"Do you have someplace to live? Someone to take care of you? I see you didn't list any address."

"They might come back, so I can't go there."

"Where is that?"

"The red place."

Margo looked away from the pathetic creature before her and gazed for a moment at the calendar on the cubicle wall. It was from a local Chinese restaurant and showed a picture of a coy Asian woman standing in front of a garden, holding a parasol. Chinese cheesecake, Margo thought. She had to move on, there was a waiting room full of desperate people.

"I think you need to stay here for the night, but it's going to be some time before we can find a bed for you. I'm sure you can rest on one of the cots in back for now." The emergency-room doctor had decided against keeping the patient overnight in the hospital. Margo knew this was mainly because of a lack of available beds. Especially for the nut cases. She decided to shift Susan Doe over to the psych ward. At least there, someone would keep an eye on her.

Susan was riffling through her pockets. "I lost my bag. My stuff. I don't know. Do you have a cigarette?"

"I'm sorry, I don't smoke."

"Shit. Fuck. Excuse me, I can see you're a real lady." There was sarcasm in her tone. Margo was glad to end the interview.

"Not really. Now, if you'll just go take a seat, I'll write out the recommendation and we'll find you a bed."

Susan was taking things out of her pocket. A dirty lipstick case. A piece of crumpled tissue. A pack of matches.

Jack's Café-Bar, Amsterdam Avenue.

Margo looked at the familiar logo, startled.

"Why, that's—" She stopped herself. It was never good to reveal anything personal to a patient. The woman snatched the matches off the table, stared hard at Margo and walked out.

Strange, Margo thought now, rereading the file in the privacy of her apartment. She had written, in her small, slanted hand: "paranoid delusions" and "probable drug abuser" and "hospitalization recommended," but Susan Doe had vanished long before they ever found a bed for her, out into the night or the dawn, another soul adrift.

She picked up the next file. Glancing at the

clock in the living room, she was surprised to see that it was after two and she was getting tired at last. She went into the kitchen and heated up some soy milk, added honey and sipped it slowly, letting the warmth steam her face. As she passed the window, she couldn't resist a peek out. The street was empty.

All at once she heard a soft scraping sound, and the unmistakable creak of floorboards just outside her door.

She spun around, her hand flying up to her throat in some kind of instinctive protective gesture.

Sliding under the door, ever so slowly, was a Chinese takeout menu. Then she heard the soft tread of footsteps retreating down the stairs.

"Jesus, Mary and Joseph," she breathed, cupping her hand over her mouth to keep from laughing out loud.

She tried the television, just for the sound, flipping quickly through the channels with the remote, landing on a perfectly disgusting cable ad for escort services. She watched as the woman in the ad writhed her naked genitals at the camera and promised "I'll do anything you want, you can fuck me in the ass, my juicy pussy is waiting for you, just call 970-CUNT or 970-SLUT."

How many other people were watching this? she wondered. It was embarrassing to think about. Did men find this stuff erotic? Did they actually call up the numbers? They must, or there wouldn't be so many ads. Men were too peculiar, they were barely civilized and reverted to the wild at the slightest push, especially when they lived alone.

There was simply too much testosterone in the world, she thought, smiling as she remembered an argument she'd had with Art on the subject. She'd suggested, purely as a hypothesis, that wars might serve a societal purpose, weeding out the aggressive males. She pointed out that the last decade had been dangerously peaceful, especially in Western countries like America and Britain, where excess hormones expressed themselves in soccer riots. She was only half joking.

"Are you saying we should start a war?" Art demanded.

"No, what we need is some kind of substitute, a game or something."

"I think I saw that in a movie."

"Or a war in some place we don't care about."

"Like Vietnam?"

"Or maybe there should just be an operation at birth. Testosterectomy. Removal of excess male hormones. An adjustment of the extra Y chromosome in the womb."

She had been pretty ridiculous. It was just one of those days when she was harassed on the street once too often (once was too often) and there'd been some horrible rape all over the front pages. She could see now why Art had accused her of hating men. No, she'd insisted, meaning it, she liked them, *loved* them, but she was still afraid of them. In packs. Sometimes even alone.

At that point Art had gotten all sexy and seductive, turned her on, his edginess exciting. Maybe that was the thing about men, you never knew when they were going to go nuts on you, and that was part of the fascination. As much as she disliked his drinking, his smoking, his irresponsibility, she knew enough about herself to know that there was a part of her that vicariously liked it. His instability made him somehow controllable. And a man like that, who was never all there for anyone, was all the more tantalizing.

She took her lukewarm soy milk into the bedroom.

How can you drink that stuff? she heard Art saying.

She laughed, as if he were in the room. "Because it's good for me, of course!"

She crawled under the comforter, reached up to turn off the light, expecting to fall asleep quickly. But she was still unaccountably afraid. It came over her lately out of nowhere: a sense of her own mortality as real as the air around her, the sheets against her skin.

Forcing her mind away from the fear, she lay in the dark and counted: "One: the Montreal Expos. Two: the New York Mets. Three: the Philadelphia Phillies . . ."

Working her way down the East Coast, across the Midwest, and all the way to the San Francisco Giants, she managed to fall asleep before she reached the American League.

23

For a while, Susan was the same as any commuter at the train station. There was an orange-juice cart that had oranges like a small world of golden suns piled behind the glass.

"The blood of the sun," she warned the vendor. He snarled at her in another tongue. "Orange," she said, "death." Just a few weeks before there had been pumpkins all over: that's what people thought. She knew they were severed heads.

She left the train station before something terrible could happen, but when she got outside, the cold bit and she pulled the blanket up around her face so that she could just see out. Noise like machinery hummed inside her head, people yelling and screaming, their voices jumbled together. Sometimes a particular message came through. The other day she had clearly heard one of them say: Susan, the river. But what had it meant? The Hudson River? The East River? And it was too cold to go there now.

She wandered uptown from Penn Station toward the bus terminal, but when she got there, a disturbing vision arose of the crazies who lived in the terminal, so she kept going until she came to a bank. The alcove with the machines was lit up and heated. People stuck their cards in a slot on the door and it buzzed them in.

The same way she'd been buzzed into the social worker's building, looking for him. She had pushed all the buttons next to the mailboxes until one spoke back to her and she was inside. But she could not find him, either there or at the bar, and it was important that he see her before it was too late.

She went into the bank behind two men who were talking to each other in code and she sat on the wide, low window ledge while they put cards in the machine and got money.

". . . my own company," one man was saying, ". . . wave of the future."

The other man nodded and looked at his watch. "Listen, Bernie, I got a bus to catch."

"Just take a sec to look at this, it's incredible." Bernie opened his briefcase, a fancy one with combination locks.

If someone stole it, why wouldn't they just break it open?

They were finished with the money machines and walked over to the ledge where Susan was sitting. As if she wasn't even there.

Bernie took out a gray brochure. "Welcome to the office of the future! Enjoy tomorrow today!"

Tomorrow today. Tomorrow today. She rubbed her forehead, trying to understand.

More people buzzed into the bank's alcove. They waited in line. Stepped up to the machines that went *beep beep beep* and money came out. One machine stopped giving money and people cursed it. Every time a new person came in they tried the broken machine, thinking they would outsmart all the other people. Even when someone on the line told them it was broken, they tried it anyway, not believing.

"You see, Jay," Bernie was saying, his brows moving up and down like caterpillars, "all our old ways of doing business will soon be obsolete. With the Networker you're connected to all the information you need at any given moment by computer! Say you want to reach Joe Smith in San Francisco, you call him up, right?"

"Right," said the other man, looking at his watch again.

Their voices faded in and out, mingling with her own voices, like distant stations on a radio. She was warm now but still hurting.

"And he's not there, so his secretary takes the message and he calls you back later, but maybe now *you're* out and this goes on for days—"

She moaned softly, to test them. They didn't look at her. She really had transformed her molecules to invisibility.

More people came into the bank and went out, talking to each other in codes.

"With the Networker, you enter your 'Request.' " He pulled out a cardboard mock-up of a computer board and screen and punched at various symbols. "Type in 'Info,' the date you need it, your initials, and it's there, Joe Smith comes back, types in for his 'Mail,' sees your 'Request,' and responds with 'Affirm' or 'Search' or 'Ineligible.' "

" 'Ineligible'?"

"Means he can't do it."

"Do what?"

"Whatever you requested." Bernie smiled, showing large yellow teeth. "That's the beauty part! There are no 'maybes' in the Networker! There are Promises, Commitments, Requests, Affirms . . ."

She reached under her blanket for Joey's arsenal. The cool hard metal felt good in her hand. Solid and real.

". . . Fulfill, Invalidate, Redesign Priorities, Calendar Evaluation . . . with the twelve-sixty. . . ."

Bernie and Jay were gone and she stretched out on the window ledge.

Sometimes she forgot why she was waiting. Then remembered again.

Could a person die more than once? She didn't see how it was possible. Which meant that she could never die now. He had made her strong and forever. She had to show him, show him that she had come back new and improved. He would be so impressed.

She looked out the bank window at the cars blurring down the avenue. They caught her thoughts and took them tumbling along. Bruised her inside behind her eyes. There were gold and silver lights on the stores and restaurants, flashing off and on, and people running to catch a bus at the corner.

The machines went *beep beep beep* and spat out money.

24

When he got out of the Port Authority Bus Terminal, the icy air hit him with full force. He'd had a hint of it at the stop in Washington, D.C., stepping out of the bus to stretch his legs and find a cup of coffee and a doughnut, but that was only for a few minutes and he'd had the stuffy, steamy bus to climb back into.

It had been a grueling trip. At first, in Miami, he had a seat to himself, but as the bus wended its way north, more people got on, toting crying children, takeout fried chicken, and radios. In spite of the commotion, the smells and closeness of too much humanity, he slept a lot. He was down to his last few dollars and he couldn't buy much food but had little appetite. He was feverish, his body rising to sweating heats, then leaving him shivering with cold. In the worst of the fever, he lost track of where he was as he drifted in and out. Sometimes the bus seemed to be flying, or moving backward at a great speed. He lost track of the rest stops and the states they passed through. He'd awake with a start, unsure whether he was in a bus or a plane, still on the island or in Margo's bed in New York.

The ride in the small rattling prop plane from Eleuthera to Miami had taken half his cash, and as he'd feared, his credit cards were no good at the airlines.

"I'm sorry," drawled the airport reservations clerk, a perky Floridian whose smile revealed an expanse of upper gums. "Your VISA has been canceled." Cayunsuled. Art didn't even bother to try out the expired Amex.

He had just enough money left for a one-way bus ticket to New York.

Now he stood in the bitter November wind on the corner of Eighth Avenue and Forty-second Street at 10:30 in the morning, wearing the same soiled white shirt and slacks he'd had on when he fled the island and a thin pair of moccasins he'd bought from the fisherman. He counted his remaining money: $3.74. That would almost pay for a taxi to Jack's.

He hailed one, climbed in, and gave the club's Upper West Side address.

"Been in a fight?" the driver asked suspiciously, eyeing Art's appearance. It was a private cab, with interior decoration, a tensor lamp over the backseat, signs pasted all over: "No Smoking." "Talk to Driver About Out-of-Town

Trips." "SMILE." A Garfield cat doll was stuck upside down on the back window. Pompoms dangled from the rearview mirror.

"No. On vacation."

"Must have been quite a trip."

"It was."

"Just got back from Orlando myself," said the driver, warming up a little. "My in-laws got a place there. Near Disney World. We take the kids. How about that Epcot Center? Pretty incredible, huh? And now they got this movie-studio place. It's amazing what them Disney people can come up with, huh?"

"Yeah."

"Bet you were in someplace warm, huh? Am I right?"

"Right."

"This cold snap hit outta nowhere. Fucking freezing, ain't it? Better get yourself a warm coat 'fore you get pneumonia or something. Me, I got a down coat from L. L. Bean. Get yourself one a them."

Art was shivering, even in the warmth of the cab. As they passed Columbus Circle, the meter was already up to three dollars. He momentarily considered telling the guy he didn't have enough money.

"Look at all this," the driver was saying. "Fucking Christmas decorations already. Been up for days. The stores start earlier every year. I mean, who the hell wants to think about

Christmas already? Now we're stuck with it till January. Fucking Christmas.''

They pulled up in front of Jack's and Art immediately realized that it was closed, but he had no choice except to get out.

He handed over three dollars and seventy-four cents, although the meter said three-ninety.

"Look, I'm sorry, this is all I have. I thought it would be enough but it isn't."

The driver counted it out, frowning. Then he shrugged. "Listen, am I gonna go broke on two bits? Forget about it. Get yourself a coat."

He drove off.

Art felt tears sting his eyes, partly from the unexpected kindness of the cabdriver, partly from the cold, but mostly because Jack's was locked up tight and he had no place to go.

He would not call Margo, not until he'd gotten himself in better shape. But he couldn't just stand here, freezing to death. Jesus Christ, how had he gotten himself into such a mess? He looked up and down the block, trying to think of something to do, someone to turn to. He didn't even have the change for a cup of coffee or a phone call, let alone a pack of cigarettes.

He turned back to Jack's, as if maybe the security gates would vanish, the doors magically open for him. He grabbed hold of the cold iron bars and shook them with all his strength.

"Art?"

Jack Brady himself, all six feet four of him,

looking even larger in a nearly ankle-length fur coat, had come up behind him.

"Good Christ, Jack!"

"What the fuck are you doing, tryin' to bend the bars with your bare hands?"

"I've never been so happy to see anyone. I just got back and I'm broke, big surprise, right? And I'm kind of between apartments, and—"

"Love your outfit. This some kind of penance?" Jack opened the gates and rolled them back, fit his key into the door.

Art felt a warm blast of welcome stale air, a familiar mix of old cigarettes and beer.

"Christ, Christ," he said, slapping his arms to drive out the cold.

"Here," said Jack, tossing over his fur coat. Art wrapped himself in it.

"You don't happen to have a cigarette, do you?"

"You know I don't smoke that poison, but help yourself." He handed Art change for the cigarette machine. The clatter of the Marlboro pack was about the happiest sound Art had ever heard. He lit up, taking it in deep.

"You know," Jack was saying as he unlocked his small private office, "I only came in to get last night's receipts. This is probably only the second time this year I left them till the next day, but me and the wife had a family thing to go to yesterday, out on the island, and didn't get back till late, so I had Gordie lock it all up.

Otherwise, you'd still be freezin' your butt off out there."

"There is a God."

Jack looked at him. "I wonder."

"Oh, fuck, fuck, what a fucked-up mess."

"Have a nice trip?"

"Jesus H. Christ on a fucking pogo stick. Jesus Horatio Christ. I need a drink."

"You need a bath and a meal, I'd say."

"Yeah, yeah, you're right. I better check in somewhere. Listen, you wouldn't mind advancing me—"

Jack had already taken the money out of the till. He handed Art two hundred dollars. "Art Glenn, you're so far into the company store, I've bought your soul ten times over."

"Just don't try to resell it."

"Can you work tonight?"

"I guess. How's Mattie been working out?"

"Fine. 'Cept he has another gig tonight and he couldn't get anyone else. So your timing was good for a change."

"Listen. This is gonna sound strange, but . . . have there been any cops around asking about me?"

"No. Why? You in some kind of trouble?"

"No, no, not really. It's nothing. Guy was after me about some, uh, back rent. Said he'd take it to court. I just wondered."

Jack gave him a funny look and went into the office. He returned with Art's suitcase.

"You might need this. Those are the silliest-looking pair of shoes I've ever seen."

"Hey, my stuff! Great! Now all I need is a place to crash today."

"Oh, for Christ sake, here." Jack gave Art a set of keys. "My wife's still out on the island with her sister till tomorrow. I'm gonna be runnin' errands all day, so use the flat but don't make a mess. And show up here on time tonight."

"Jack, you're a gentleman and a scholar."

"Give me back my fur coat."

Art took it off and handed it over. He opened his suitcase and put on two sweaters, a pair of socks, and his old sneakers.

He figured it would be better to go to the police the next day, when he was cleaned up and rested and didn't look like a bum. He bought a newspaper on the way to Jack's apartment, not really expecting to see anything about the death of some woman on the Lower East Side that happened nearly a week ago, but if anyone would have the story, it would be the *Post*.

There was nothing and he was more relieved than he expected.

After taking a long hot shower, he fell onto Jack's couch and slept until it was time to go to work at ten. He had just enough time to throw a sandwich together out of Jack's refrigerator, realizing it was the first solid food he'd had in days, the first he'd wanted.

He promised himself that this was a new start

for him. He'd quit drinking, and even smoking. He'd make things up with Margo and live like a normal human being. Maybe they'd even get married and have a family. And pets, they'd have pets, too. And a great apartment they'd figure out a way to buy. Oh, yes, things were going to be different, now.

25

People were really happy to see him. Even though it seemed as if they never listened to his playing, when he wasn't there they missed him. Go figure. Mattie was okay, but he played too many show tunes, one of the regulars confided, leaning drunkenly over the piano.

The place was crowded, with that spirit the club got early in the holiday season, when everyone spent money and stayed out late. Before they were broke from buying presents for people they wouldn't even know the next year, and went to too many disappointing parties. It didn't take long for the novelty of Art's return to wear off and everyone got as noisy as always, but he didn't care. He was happy to be somewhere that felt a little like home.

And then, to lift him even higher, Margo appeared.

He caught her gaze and smiled. It was a real

movie moment, the kind of rush that makes all the shit worthwhile.

She sat down at the bar and took off her coat. He saw she was wearing a sheer white blouse that seemed to shimmer in the light, and clingy red slacks. She sipped a glass of wine as she watched him and he basked in the attention, playing effortlessly, only stopping between songs for a sip of whiskey—after all, he had a lot to celebrate, so he'd stop drinking tomorrow.

When the set was over, he went straight to her. They just stood there, looking at each other, almost afraid to touch. He broke the moment by taking her gently in his arms.

She whispered in his ear, "I want to be in bed with you."

He touched her small wrist, turning it to look at her watch. "Another hour and a half. I don't know if I can stand it." He kissed her, right there in front of everybody. The regulars went "woo woo" and Jack bought a round of drinks. He wanted to start telling her about all the crazy things that had happened to him but didn't know where to begin, so he decided he'd wait until later, when they were alone and after they'd made love a few times. He needed an avalanche of pure sensation to restore him, to reassure himself that everything would be all right now.

As he played again, he went over in his mind the story he would relate to Margo: the horrible accident, the boat, the island, his flight from the dogs. He could hardly believe it wasn't a night-mare, but he had cuts on his feet to prove it.

At 1:30, Jack said get the hell home. He couldn't bear to watch the yearning looks that were passing between Art and Margo, and he sent them off with a toast, like newlyweds.

In the cab down to her place, they held each other without speaking, kissed so long and hard they didn't notice the cab had stopped.

"Jesus, I love you," he said as they went into her vestibule. Margo fumbled with the key, finally got it in the door, and they went up the stairs clinging together. At the fourth landing, Margo's floor, one of two hall lights was out.

"Damn," said Margo, squinting at the key-hole.

There was no way to see the person hiding in the shadows until she stepped down from the stairs that led to the roof, a strange figure in a tattered blanket. Her eyes seemed locked in a peculiar stare.

Margo recognized her immediately, even in the dim light. She was good at faces, and she'd just been going over the woman's file two nights before. She immediately assumed the woman had tracked her down because she needed Margo's help. It wouldn't be the first time a patient had found her at home.

Art went rigid with shock. Margo turned to him and was startled by the transformation. He had an expression of horror on his face, as if he were confronting a ghost. He looked so sickly that Margo was afraid for him, but the distraught woman clearly needed her help, too.

Susan gripped Joey's arsenal the way people did on television. She knew that it was not the gun but her eyes that could really hurt him, and she pushed out beams like bolts of lightning. She wished the social worker would get the hell out of the way.

"No, it's okay, Art, I know her," Margo said, turning to the woman. "Susan, right?"

When he saw the gun, he acted instinctively, pulling Margo to the side and behind him.

Then Margo saw the gun, too, and looked from it to the woman's face. The blanket had fallen to her shoulders, revealing the soiled bandages.

"Look, you don't want to hurt anyone," Margo whispered.

The woman ignored her, staring at Art. She said in a monotone, "You just left me there."

"No, no, I didn't mean to. Really!"

"I don't understand," said Margo, stepping forward, her hand out as if to placate a wild animal.

The gun went off then, a huge sound in the small space. Margo heard it with a split second of wonder that such a thing could happen. She felt searing pain and saw the heat of a vast bright light geysering up and up, breaking into billions of tiny wriggling fireworks, the pieces of her life and fragments of her memory, blinking out one by one until there was nothing left but darkness.

She went limp against Art and crumpled slowly to the floor, blood spreading over her white blouse.

Susan paused for just a second, confused.

Art grabbed the gun. He seized the barrel and twisted it around. She fought him with surprising strength, and it flashed through his mind that he could lose and he was going to die, but he managed to get the gun high up over their heads. He was so close to her he could feel her breath on his cheek. She never took her eyes off him, growling low in her throat as they struggled, a keening that rose to a high-pitched howl of rage as Art turned the gun around with a sudden jolt. He slammed the barrel against her temple and squeezed his hand over her fingers gripping the trigger. She screamed and he heard the crack of bone. He kept squeezing until the trigger gave. The explosion shattered the side of her face, sending a spray of blood and bone against the wall. She veered back toward the stair railing, her face and skull a mass of gore, the gun still in her hand. Her body teetered on the rail and Art lifted his foot and pushed at her chest with his shoe, toppling her. Her body thudded down the stairs and came to rest on the next landing.

Art was panting hard, his fists gripped tight. He wanted to kill her again. He wanted to bring her back to life just so he could kill her again.

The neighbors were coming out, in robes and pajamas. There were screams and commotion. Someone yelled that they were calling the police.

Art dropped to his knees beside Margo. He touched her pale face and thought he saw her eyelids flutter, but there was no other movement.

"It'll be okay," he told her softly. "And I'll never go away again. Just you be okay."

Even when the EMS workers had pulled the white sheet over her face, he wouldn't believe it.

The police were swarming around, asking him questions. They helped him down the stairs. Someone draped a blanket over his shoulders.

There were so many lights, it was like they were making a movie on the street. Police cars, their top lights spinning in dizzying circles; two ambulances; a truck marked "City Mortuary." Even a news van had found its way there; the reporters were already interviewing the neighbors. People leaned out the windows staring with curious and bored expressions at the live entertainment that had come to their block.

Just before he got into the police car, he stopped and looked up at Margo's apartment window, as if she might be there, waiting for him. She had to be because there was so much he needed to tell her and he had come such a long way.

EPILOGUE

He could not feel the room turning and only knew that it was when he looked up every so often. The supper club high atop a skyscraper was walled-in glass, and as the entire floor rotated imperceptibly, it offered different views of the city. For a few songs he faced the Hudson River, then the downtown caverns, and before he knew it, he was looking at the glittering necklaces that were the East Side bridges.

The room was hushed and distinctly elegant, a place where people came to listen, to sigh over the music and pull a lover or spouse closer. He sang the most beautiful songs, in an understated style the critics had fallen in love with. They adored the contrast between his sweet, sad music and the front-page notoriety that had brought him to their attention in the first place.

For a while it seemed as if he would never get off the front pages. But after the inquest and the lack of charges, interest died down in the shocking story of the street woman who had killed her social worker and herself, and of the heartbroken lover who had been unable to stop the tragedy from happening. His being a musician had spiced it up, tugging hearts all over the city.

He would work only until twelve and go home alone. There was a recording session in the morning and he wanted to play his best.